Lily

The Highland Clan
BOOK THREE

KEIRA MONTCLAIR

THE GRANTS AND RAMSAYS IN 1280'S

Grants

1. Laird Alexander Grant, and wife, Maddie (Book #1 of Clan Grant)
   a. Twin lads-James (Jamie) and John (Jake)
   b. Kyla
   c. Connor
   d. Elizabeth

2. Brenna Grant and husband, Quade Ramsay (Book #2 of Clan Grant)
   a. Torrian (Quade's son from first marriage) and wife, Heather, daughter, Nellie (Book #2 of the Highland Clan)
   b. Lily (Quade's daughter from first marriage)
   c. Bethia
   d. Gregor
   e. Jennet

3. Robbie Grant and wife, Caralyn (Book #4 of Clan Grant)
   a. Ashlyn (Caralyn's daughter from a previous relationship)
   b. Gracie (Caralyn's daughter from a previous relationship)
   c. Rodric (Roddy)
   d. Padraig

4. Brodie Grant and wife, Celestina (Book #3 of Clan Grant)
   a. Loki (adopted) and Arabella-son, Lucas (Book One of The Highland Clan)
   b. Braden
   c. Catriona
   d. Alison

5. Jennie Grant and husband, Aedan Cameron (Book #7 of Clan Grant)
   a. Riley
   b. Tara
   c. Brin

Ramsays

1. Quade Ramsay and wife, Brenna Grant (see above)

2. Logan Ramsay and wife, Gwyneth (Book #5 of Clan Grant)
a. Molly (adopted)
b. Maggie (adopted)
c. Sorcha
d. Gavin
e. Brigid

3. Micheil Ramsay and wife, Diana (Book #6 of Clan Grant)
a. David
b. Daniel

4. Avelina Ramsay and Drew Menzie (Book #8 of Clan Grant)
a. Elyse
b. Tad
c. Tomag
d. Maitland

CHAPTER ONE

1280s, Scotland

Lily Ramsay froze, afraid to move. She'd heard a sound that had crept up her spine and run through every golden hair attached to her head. Someone or something was watching her.

She should have known better than to wander this far into the forest. Her sire and stepmother had warned her multiple times against going off on her own. She was the Ramsay chieftain's sister, which made her a likely target, but she'd chosen to ignore her parents' advice.

How she wished she'd listened. Closing her eyes, she stood tall and swung both arms up over her head, reaching toward the sky, and then brought them down in a slow, calming movement. She sucked in a deep breath and let it out.

Once she felt better, Lily glanced to her left, in the direction the sound had come from, but neither a single pine needle nor blade of grass moved. Moving in the opposite direction, she placed one foot in front of the other, singing her stepmama's favorite song in her head.

Thankfully, this was also the way back toward the safety of the castle. She'd ridden farther than she'd intended while chasing after that wounded fox. Of course, he had disappeared the moment he entered the forest. Lily had lost him in the time it took to dismount her beloved horse, Sunshine. How many times had she been chastised for her wandering mind, her forgetfulness, and her free spirit? No matter how hard she tried, she could not help but be distracted by all the beauty of nature and God's wondrous creatures, especially those in need of help. Alas, the fox was nowhere to be seen, so it was time to return home.

She counted her steps just as her stepmama had taught her to do to keep her mind focused on the task at hand.

The sound of a twig snapping behind her hit her like the hilt of a sword, warning her. Was it an animal or a person? She increased her pace to a run as she peered over her shoulder, but there was nothing there.

The sound and sensation of brush and tree branches hitting her face and arms reminded her to slow down. If she didn't, she wouldn't hear the approach of whatever or whoever was tracking her.

Why had she wandered so far away from safety? She recalled the trickery she'd used to get past the guards at the gate—how she'd promised to go for a short ride, within their eyesight, and be right back. How could she have known a fox would distract her? Mounting her horse, she'd flicked the reins and smiled sweetly at the three guards, knowing they'd do that foolish thing all the lads did when she smiled at them. They'd stared at her, mouths smiling widely, unable to tear their gazes from her as she flew across the meadow on her beloved horse, Sunshine. They must have discovered her ruse, of course, but by then she was too far gone for them to catch her.

But none of that mattered now—all that mattered was this headlong flight. Finally breaking out of the thick copse of trees into the clearing, she almost breathed a sigh of relief, knowing her horse was just ahead. And then her stomach dropped to her toes in an instant.

Her horse was gone.

"Sunshine? Sunshine?" She searched the area, hoping her beloved friend was hiding, but the mare was nowhere to be found. Lily swung around in a circle, but saw nothing to aid her. And the rustling in the bushes had returned.

Stop! You're overset with all your worry. There is naught there.

Much as she tried to convince herself, she failed, because *something was there.* Her senses did not oft steer her wrong. Spinning around, she flew off into the distance toward the keep, hiking up her skirts and running as fast as she could.

Why had she been so foolish? Aye, Lily felt abandoned by her brother, Torrian, now that he spent all his leisure time with his sweet wife, Heather, and aye, she feared she was no longer of value to the clan now that Heather had taken over her duties. But that was no reason to ignore all the teachings her sire had instilled in her for years.

Lily tore through the forest as fast as she could, gasping for air. "Help! Someone please help!"

The sounds behind her continued to get louder and closer. She glanced over her shoulder to see a man in chain mail. Blood raced through her body, urging her onward—faster, faster.

"Stop!" His voice carried a long distance because it was so deep and menacing.

Lily screamed louder and louder and louder.

Afraid to look back again, but forcing herself, she closed her eyes and rotated her head, peeking just for an instant.

There was no questioning it—he was following her. The helm on his head showed only a fringe of brown hair sticking out of the bottom, concealing his identity completely. The heavy chain mail on his trunk slowed him, but not enough. Tears slid down her cheeks, dripping over her chin as she ran. She would never make it to the keep, and there was nowhere else to go. The open meadow in front of her offered no hiding places, no warriors to save her, no guardsmen to ride their horses toward her.

It was hopeless. He'd catch her for sure and…and…

Her arms windmilled around her as her fear made every hair on her skin stand at attention.

"Lily. Stop."

She squeaked at the sound of her name. "Leave me be. Go away."

Nothing could have encouraged her to run faster than a stranger in armor yelling at her. She did not know him for certes; she would have recognized his voice. He was not of the Ramsay clan. He wore nothing to identify him as most Scots did.

She could just make out the large sword sheathed over his shoulder.

"Lily, please. I want to take care of you."

He must be getting closer because she could feel the ground vibrating beneath her from his heavy footfalls.

"Save me, please. Someone help me." Her terror caught her next scream in her throat and she gagged, coughing and spitting at the same time, causing her to trip and almost lose her footing. But she caught herself and continued onward, her lungs screaming for mercy as they fought for every bit of air she could get.

Her stomach spasmed with fear. *Please, God. Save me. Please Mama, help me.* Glancing back at her pursuer again, she allowed herself to feel a moment of gratitude for his armor. If he had not been wearing it, he would have caught her by now. That same muffled voice reached her ears.

"Stop, I say. Stop!"

Her legs twisted in her skirts and she stumbled, catching herself with her hand before she sprawled across the ground. As soon as she picked herself back up, she started running once more, screaming and yelling as she went, her entire being frantic.

She rounded a group of trees and blinked twice in relief when she saw the Ramsay castle in the distance. Mayhap there was now hope for her. She had to outrun him, she just had to.

"Stop. I love you. Just stop!"

Lily's eyes widened at the lad's crazed declaration. In love with her? Who would yell such a thing while in frantic pursuit of her? The sound of boots crunching on the stones of the Highlands grew louder and louder. What would he do when he caught her? If he fell on her in his present clothing, he'd crush her for sure.

Closer…

Please God, I'll never be foolish again. I'll do as my sire advised. I'll not run off on my own. Please save me from this unknown monster.

"Help me, please! Someone help me!" she screamed. He was almost upon her. "Nay, nay, save me!" A quick glance over her shoulder was all she needed to confirm he was bearing down on her.

In the distance, a lone horseman appeared from the castle. She wished to stop to catch her breath, but could not. She swung her arms wildly over her head, hoping that the person saw her, hoping she was the reason they were in full gallop.

As she ran toward the horseman, she dared another quick glance behind her. Tears of relief streamed down her face. The man in armor was retreating, disappearing into the trees. Moments later, she saw him riding off into the distance.

It did not change the fear that held an iron grip on her. She raced toward the horseman in the blue Ramsay plaid, not knowing who it was, not caring either.

Once the warrior drew near, she recognized him, his long dark hair waving behind him as he rode. "Kyle, thank the heavens above, Kyle. You saved me." She held her arms up to him, but not before she swiped all the tears off her face.

"Where the devil is your horse, Lily? You came out this far alone, walking? What has possessed you to be so careless?"

"Sunshine is gone. I know not where she went. Please, Kyle, do not yell at me. Can you not see how upset I am? Just help me." Lily's breath hitched as she stared up into his deep blue eyes.

Kyle grabbed her by the waist and lifted her onto the horse in front of him so she faced him. Once she was situated, he dropped the reins to wrap his arms around her and she threw herself at him, clinging to him and sobbing into his shoulder. "Oh, Kyle, I was so frightened." She played with the threads in his sleeve, sniffing more than she needed to so she could take in Kyle's comforting scent.

"What has possessed you of late? Your brother will probably whip the guards for allowing you out on your own. You need to stop talking sweet to our lads. They make poor decisions when you are about. 'Tis about the tenth lad you've used your trickery on this week. 'Tis a good thing I keep watch for you. As soon as I came out of your brother's solar, I noticed you were missing. Who knows where you'd be now if I had not searched you out?"

Lily sobbed even harder, realizing every word Kyle spoke was true. She could use her trickery to get past any of the guards, and she oft did. It was wrong, and she knew it, but now that Heather had control over the stores and the kitchens, she worried she was no longer needed. Though she loved Heather with all her heart, and it was undeniable that her new sister was much better at numbers, losing her duties—and her brother's attention—had left a void in her.

No one cared about her anymore. Why, she'd just proved it, had she not? She'd left the castle unescorted and no one had cared.

Only Kyle. She hitched her breath three more times and sobbed into his shoulder even harder, drenching his plaid for sure.

Kyle Maule would wring the lass's wee neck. She was beautiful, aye, but he was not fool enough to allow Lily the chance to do as she liked. He had vowed to Torrian Ramsay, his friend and laird, that he would protect her, and at present, he would wager he'd probably lose his life doing it, lovely trickster that she was.

Ever since Torrian had married and taken over as chieftain of the Ramsay clan, Lily had been unsettled. Kyle was also in a new position as second to the chieftain of the Ramsay clan, so he had many new responsibilities. It heartened him to know that if his sire could see him now, he'd be proud of him. Kyle could not risk losing this position. He'd worked too hard to get it, and he would do anything for his clan.

He turned his horse around and headed back to the castle, still holding Lily as she cried. "Lily, you must exercise more caution."

She continued to blubber on, bits and pieces of sentences catching his ear...*no use...no value, no one cares, almost kidnapped.* His tunic was drenched through from her tears, and he was grateful it was autumn and not mid-winter. Memories of Lily planting a kiss on his lips surfaced in the forefront of his mind. She'd run out of Torrian's chieftain ceremony a few moons ago, and he'd followed her to see what ailed her.

He'd had no idea that she would kiss him, and worse yet, that she would taste so good. He'd kissed many lasses, but Lily? He'd lost his head completely and kissed her back, parting her lips with his tongue so he could really taste her.

And that delicious taste had never left him. It tormented him day and night. Aye, every bit of Lily Ramsay was sweet, but would his laird accept a warrior's suit for his sister? He doubted it. At any rate, he was too busy with his new job to offer for the sweet lass, though she was making it more and more difficult for him to ignore her.

She leaned back to stare into his eyes as he managed to get his horse turned around and trotting back toward the castle. "Who could it have been? Who would wish to hurt me?"

"I have no idea, Lily. I saw someone on horseback, but he was not near you, and by the time I reached you, he was gone. But must I remind you how many times you've been advised not to wander alone? You put yourself in danger."

"But I'm not the chieftain's daughter any more, I'm just his sister. No one cares. And please do not tell my sire or brother about this. I promise not to use trickery again."

"Lily, if the man was after you, I must tell them both. We must send guards out to patrol the area. I will not keep this from them."

His words finally managed to sink into her brain. "Kyle, you must have gotten a good look, did you not? I did not see him in the forest, I just heard the rustling. But as soon as I started running, he followed me. He was a man dressed all in armor...and...and he said he *loved* me. He almost caught me. Then he saw you and jumped on his horse and left. Who could it have been?" She ran her hands up and down his forearms as she spoke.

Must she continue to touch him so? He could not concentrate on her words when her hands were on him. He let out a low growl, then stopped himself, scowling because he'd let her hear his reaction to her. "I did not notice he was in chain mail, but he was a good distance away." True, when Lily was within range, he usually could see naught but Lily. He had tried to stop this foolish attraction since it was unlikely anything could come of it, but the more he tried to stop it, the more distracted he became. Had he been so distracted that he had missed something important? Had the horseman threatened Lily? He growled again.

"Why are you making that funny sound, Kyle?" She peered at him with a strange expression.

Blast! She'd heard it. "What sound?" he asked, trying to look puzzled.

"You sounded like a wild bear just now. Are you angry with me?"

She batted her eyelashes at him, and he narrowed his gaze at her, hoping it would be enough for her to drop the subject.

"Why do you glare so, Kyle? Do you not like me any longer? Are you like the others?"

He growled in frustration. "Lily, you speak nonsense. Everyone loves you and you are fully aware of it. What is this game you play?"

"I do not know of what you speak." Her chin lifted and her lower lip protruded.

And if she moved in any closer to him, he wouldn't be able to stop himself from nibbling that lower lip. He closed his eyes to block out the sweet temptation, but then decided that wasn't such a good idea since they were on horseback. As soon as she started to wiggle, his eyes flew open again.

"What is it now, lass?" His eyes widened. Would her endless taunting never cease? Did she not understand what she did to him?

Her lower lip trembled. "You are mad at me. You are always angry with me, shouting at me. No one ever shouts at me the way you do."

"Of course I shout at you," he bellowed. "Who is the one charged with your safety? You always disregard everyone's advice and do as you wish. Someone must keep watch over you."

She stuck her lower lip out a bit more. "My father *used to* watch over me."

"He has a bad knee! He can barely walk on good days."

"My brother *used to* watch over me."

If she whined any louder, his ears would hurt. "He's the new chieftain, and if you have not noticed, he has a new wife and daughter."

Frowning at him, she turned in the saddle, pushing against him until she was able to maneuver herself so she sat facing forward.

"What the hell?" he shouted.

She wiggled her bottom against him, torturing him. He tried to grab her hips to keep from throwing the horse off, but she slapped at his hand. "If you must know, I *have* noticed my brother's situation. Take me home, Kyle Maule. And do not think of taking advantage of me."

She crossed her arms in front of her and pushed away from him, her back as stiff as his cock at the moment. He ran his hand down his face in frustration. Then she lost her balance, her arms flailing as she fell back against him with an "oof," and he said a quick prayer to the Lord for patience.

The lass he loved would be the death of him yet.

CHAPTER TWO

Lily strolled through the bailey mid-morning the following day. It annoyed her to think about how her rescue from the armored man had ended. Kyle had dismounted at the stables and attempted to help her down, but she'd shove his hands aside and jumped off on her own. Her luck being what it was, her legs had buckled the moment they hit the ground and she'd fallen against him anyway.

The problem was that while Lily had told him not to touch her, she desperately wanted him to do so. Kyle Maule was the only lad who interested her, but the feeling was clearly not mutual. He'd gone out of his way to avoid her ever since the kiss they'd shared during Torrian's chieftain ceremony. Well, she was on her way out to the lists to speak to him again. Perhaps he had recalled something about the man who had chased her. Aye, that was it exactly. She needed a sound reason to go visit him so he wouldn't guess the true reason. The true reason was simple.

She missed him, and after being so unsettled yesterday, she needed some kind words from him, especially since Sunshine had not turned up yet. She was so lost without her horse, she could not spend the day without Kyle either.

Yesterday had not helped his feelings for her. She noticed he'd kept his distance from her after they'd returned to the keep. Did he not ever do anything to relax, to enjoy each special day? Now he only came after her to yell at her. And yell he had. She flipped her skirts from side to side as she strode through the courtyard, annoyed by the mere thought of how he'd chastised her. It was not her fault some fool had decided to chase her out in the meadow.

"Good morn to you, sweet Lily," the armorer said. "Glad to see you safe."

"Many thanks to you, Fergus." She smiled and gave him a slight bow. He was a sweet, hard-working man.

She came upon three lads heading out to the lists. Their names escaped her at the moment, but she halted to greet them.

"My lady, you are lovely today." The first lad walked into the second lad because he was not watching his path.

The second lad shoved at him. "Lady Lily, you are the prettiest of all the lasses in the land of the Scots."

The third one beamed at her. "Nay, you're the most beautiful in all of England." He stared at her as she strolled by them, smiling at each in passing. She appreciated how hard they worked in the lists for her brother and her sire.

"You lads are too kind to say such sweet things about me. Thank you for working so hard to protect our clan." She blushed and continued past them, noticing that the third lad was not following his mates. It was as if someone had nailed his feet to the spot.

His friend ran back and slugged him in the shoulder. "Come along, lad. Kyle will make us *all* stay longer if you dally. My pardon, Lady Lily, but we must move on."

She continued on past the buildings in the bailey, hoping to catch a quick view of Kyle, but she guessed he was already in the lists working with the men. She liked to walk past the lists on warm days, when all of the men had their shirts off. Kyle had the nicest chest of all. Strong and muscular, just the right amount of chest hair, which, of course, was as dark as the thick hair on his head. She wondered what her golden hair would look like splayed across his—

"Why, my lady, 'tis nice to see you safely back on our lands."

She jerked her head around to the carpenter who had spoken to her. "And 'tis nice to be back amongst my fine clanmates." She gave him her widest smile, hoping it would hide the blush that had spread across her cheeks at being interrupted in the middle of her carnal thoughts about Kyle.

One of the lads chased after her when she passed the stables. "My lady, where are you headed?"

"I thought I'd go to the lists to visit my brother. I'm quite sure Gregor is in the field with Kyle. Which field are they in?"

The lad's face lit up. "Why, they're just outside the castle wall today. Shall I escort you?"

She turned and curtsied to the young boy. "Why thank you, Eian. I'm sure I can find my way on my own."

After pausing to wave at the guards, she continued on her way.

"Get out of my way, I cannot see," one of them yelled to another.

A second replied, "Hellfire, nay. I want to see."

"You always get to watch her. 'Tis my turn. Now move. She likes me better."

The sound of flesh hitting flesh reached her, causing her to scowl, something she rarely did outside the privacy of her own chamber. Well, that was no longer a true statement. She did scowl around Kyle frequently, but it was all his fault.

She continued on her way, not interested in taking the time to determine what the lads at the gate were arguing about. They must have a crush on the same lass was her best guess. Who could it be? As she began to run through the possibilities, her heartbeat sped up suddenly and she slowed her steps.

Kyle. There he was at the end of the line of warriors practicing their maneuvers. His shirt was off again, just as she'd hoped. She sighed, not caring who heard her, and headed down the line of men to speak to him. She passed her brother along the way, giving him a quick wave of her hand. "Good morn to you, Gregor."

Gregor nodded but continued on with his training.

Oblivious to the others around her except the occasional shouts of "Ow!" or "Watch out!" or "Look where you're going," she continued onward until she reached her destination. Once there, she folded her hands in front of her and smiled. "Good morn to you, Kyle. Might I have a word?"

Kyle yanked his helm off and glowered at her. "Lily, why must you come all the way out here? Look at what you do to my men!"

She frowned again, though this time it was true to nature: Kyle had spoken to her. She forced the scowl away. "Whatever do you mean, Kyle? I have not said one word to any of your men. I try my verra best not to interfere with your training of the guards."

He rolled his eyes. "You do not have to speak to them to upset their concentration. Look at them." He waved his hand behind her.

She tried her best to listen to him, but she could not concentrate while standing this close to Kyle's bare chest. She licked her lips without thinking as she stared at his bare flesh—the light shining off a trickle of sweat trailing off his breastbone. She glanced up at him, and for some unknown reason she found herself enjoying the fact that she had to look up at him to meet his eyes. She squelched a sigh at how broad his shoulders were, especially when he clenched his arms so his muscles rippled in response. Aye, she enjoyed the manly display in front of her. How was she supposed to be able to think proper when he was this close to her? The hair on his head was a dark, disheveled mess, yet she'd never seen him so enticing before.

After much effort, she managed to tear her gaze away and glance over her shoulder at the line of lads she'd just passed. They were all staring at her with weak grins and distant looks.

"Do you not see what I mean?" Kyle asked, his voice was now a whisper that sent shivers down her spine.

She perused the group of them again. "Aye, but whatever are they staring at?"

"What are they looking at?" Kyle huffed the words out in apparent exasperation as he dropped his sword to the ground. "Surely, you cannot mean that. You, they're all looking at *you*." His voice had grown to a shout.

"Why are they looking at me?" she whispered, rubbing the base of her chin.

"Arghhhh…Lily! Can you not see that half of them are now bleeding because of you? Your presence distracts them. Go away, lass!"

Her lower lip trembled as she swung back to face him. "There you go, yelling at me again, Kyle Maule. Fiddle on you. I'll not tell you why I came out here, though I felt I needed to thank you for saving me."

"You thanked me yesterday, Lily. Now hasten your leave, please."

Lily scowled at him again, pursing her lips in a distinct pout. Hellfire, why did he make her scowl so? She hardly ever scowled unless he was nearby, she swore. "Mayhap I did tell you yesterday, but I have been so busy that it completely escaped my mind. I was just trying to do the proper thing. Foolish me for trying to be nice." Her hands settled on her hips and she leaned toward him, wishing she could throttle him in front of his men.

"Busy? And what is it that has kept you so busy?"

He did his best to hide his grin, but she caught it and vowed he'd regret it. "Do not dare make fun of me. I have plenty to do." She pointed her finger at his chest, wishing she would slip and land once more against that expansive piece of flesh, then lifted her chin and spun on her heel. "I'll not stay here for any more of your insults, Kyle." She flounced her skirts about her and left, but not before taking the time to smile at all the guards on her way past them. Had he spoken the truth? She did notice a few fresh injuries as she meandered past the men.

But why would they stare at her?

Kyle yelled at her retreating back. "Why do you not go help Lady Brenna? She's going to need to tend to these injuries, and they're mostly your fault."

She swiveled about, flashing a smile at the guards who were still staring at her, and bent over to pick up a handful of dirt. Then she flung it at Kyle, and he ducked, chuckling at her.

She stalked off as best she could, her boots falling into small holes as she walked, her eyes misting because everything Kyle had said was true. She had naught to do.

Naught.

Hellfire, but he'd almost cut his own hand off at the sight of the wee nymph strolling down the line of his warriors, just a heartbeat away from a stray sword. He watched her sweet backside as she stormed off, her foot catching in the ground. It took every bit of restraint he had not to chase after her, scoop her up in his arms, and take her to the stables where a fresh mound of straw was sure to be found somewhere.

He closed his eyes in the hopes it would block out the traitorous thoughts. If he did not get her off his mind, he'd lose this position he'd worked so hard to achieve. He barked to his men, "Get back to your training unless you have an injury that requires tending."

Three lads ran forward. "I'll escort Lady Lily back, then I'll stop to see what Lady Brenna says about the wound on my arm…"

Another elbowed him. "Hell, nay! I'll escort Lady Lily back. She needs a man, not a wee laddie like you."

Kyle tossed his head back and bellowed, "None of you will be escorting Lady Lily anywhere! Get back to your positions. And those who allowed themselves to be distracted by her pretty face will have to parry with me before leaving the fields."

He heard plenty of grumbling, and saw more than one surprised look. Aye, he knew it appeared he was staking a claim for Lady Lily, but how foolish could they be? She was a Ramsay chieftain's daughter. He'd never measure up to their standards. He was only the son of a guard. She could do much better than Kyle Maule.

Still, he could not allow them to get away with staring at Lily so. He'd trounce each one of them for daring to look at the sweet lass as if she were no better than a harlot.

Kyle groaned and ran his hand down his face, wiping up the sweat dripping down his brow and his cheeks. Truthfully, he could not blame them. They were no different from any of the other lads in the clan. They all wanted Lady Lily, and fortunately for his sanity, she favored none of them. But soon he feared she'd be betrothed. Torrian had mentioned it was time.

He'd go mad to see her betrothed to another.

He had to go after her, if only to tell her the happy news he'd forgotten the moment he saw her. "Gregor, you're in charge for a few moments," he yelled over to Torrian's brother. "I shall return soon."

Sheathing his sword, he hurried his steps and followed Lily back through the gates and toward the keep. She stopped to speak to everyone she met along the way, smiling and talking sweetly with them before walking onward with a bounce in her step—the very behavior that had made her the heart and soul of the Ramsay clan. But while she was beloved by all, she had no idea of her own value.

Now that Torrian was married and duties had shifted, Lily thought she had naught to do. How could she believe such a thing? Every member of the clan thrived on her presence. They delighted in her sweet smiles, her kind and genuine heart, and her thoughtful conversation.

Indeed, Lily was such a big part of Ramsay life that he knew he did not stand a chance with her. He could never measure up. Plus, he needed to concentrate on being the best possible second to the Ramsay chieftain, not drooling over the chieftain's sweet sister. He could practically hear his father telling him so over his shoulder.

As if she sensed he was behind her, Lily spun around and stared straight into his gaze. Her eyes were as green as the forest, which never failed to enchant him. "What is it, Kyle? Are you hurt?" Her hand clasped to her chest.

Hellfire, but he'd love that hand to be on his chest. Forcing himself to concentrate, he answered, "Nay, but I forgot to tell you that we found your horse outside the gates this morn."

Her eyes sparkled, and she clapped her hands, racing toward him. "You did? Truly? My Sunshine? Where is she? I must go to her."

"I'll take you." Kyle held his hand out to her and she placed hers in it. It seemed an intimacy to have her wee hand in his, and he treasured it. He didn't tell her how he'd sent dozens of his men out in search of her beloved horse yesterday, or how he'd combed the area himself late into the night after everyone else had retired to their pallets. *He* was the one who'd found Sunshine lying in the grass exhausted. After talking sweet to her and feeding her an apple, he'd managed to coax her back.

"Kyle, how could you forget such important news? I've missed my Sunshine so much. Do you not know how she lights up my day? Every day? I suppose you cannot understand such a thing, can you?"

He nodded. "Actually, I do understand." That was exactly what the sight of Lily Ramsay did to him each day—not that he would admit it to anyone. She was his type of sunshine, all by herself.

"Why? Do you have a favorite horse? Is there one special horse that lights up your day? Which one is it? It must be the fine chestnut colored one. Am I right? Am I?"

Lily had to run to keep up with him, so he slowed his steps, but she was so excited that it didn't seem to matter to her. Kyle couldn't take his gaze from her as she skipped and ran all the way to the stable.

Kyle held the door open for her when they arrived. "She was verra tired and dirty, but she showed no major distress or injury. I had the lads comb her down, get her some oats. She rested right after that." As had he, once he'd finally succumbed to exhaustion.

They moved down the stable to the last stall, the one reserved for special circumstances with its own door to the outside. As soon as Lily caught sight of her beloved white horse, she raced ahead of him. "Sunshine! My sweet Sunshine. Are you all right?" The white horse nickered as she edged over to Lily and nuzzled her neck. Lily threw her arms around the mare's neck in a hug. "Oh dear, look at your braid. The ribbons are almost out. I shall have to fix them later." She ran her hand down Sunshine's mane, straightening the matted spots the best she could. Then she hugged her horse again, her face alight with sheer joy. "You are a bit dirty, Sunshine, but I'll clean you until you sparkle."

Watching Lily like this was sure to drive him quite mad. What he would not give to trade places with that lucky horse...

Lily gushed as she petted her horse, "Oh, Sunshine, I missed you so. I'm so sorry."

She crooned and kissed her horse so much that Kyle grew hard just from imagining her kissing him like that. He turned away and she jumped, startling him.

"Oh, I must find her something sweet, I must feed her from my hand so she'll accept my apology." Lily bumped into Kyle as she chased back down the passageway in the front of the stable, shouting for the lads to find her an apple.

Kyle grunted, wondering if there was any sweeter torture than watching Lily this excited over her horse.

That damn horse. He ran his hand down his face, praying for strength, watching all the stable lads trip over one another to do her bidding.

Lily sprang back down the passageway, holding the apple out in front of her. "Look, Kyle, does this not look like the sweetest one?"

He nodded, knowing he'd never answered any question more truthfully. Aye, Lily bubbling with excitement and happiness *was* the sweetest thing he'd ever seen. She stopped next to him and said, "Here, smell it. It has the sweetest aroma." She closed her eyes and leaned close to the apple, taking in its scent and smiling. Her eyes flew open just before he was about to let out a groan. "I must give it to her so she'll forgive my carelessness yesterday."

Kyle couldn't help himself. "Och, so you admit you were careless? You should not have gone out past the guards?" He waved at the lads to go back to work and stop staring at his Lily.

Giving him a haughty look, she replied, "Kyle, I already apologized twice. Please do not ruin my reunion with my sweet horse." She shoved past him, just close enough for him to catch her enticing scent. He planned to savor it.

"I'll leave you with your horse, Lily." The torture was too much. He needed to step away.

He pivoted to leave, but stopped when he heard her say, "Kyle, wait." When he turned back, he was shocked to see she was almost upon him. She placed her hands on his still bare chest and leaned in to kiss him. "Thank you for saving my Sunshine." She placed her warm lips on his and it took all his might not to groan with pleasure.

It was a chaste kiss, but when she pulled back and stared at him, he took advantage of the moment, tugging her back. He cupped her cheeks and kissed her tenderly, because he thought that would be best for the innocent lass she was. Och, she was even more delicious than he had remembered. She leaned into him, her hands on either side of his chest, and he tucked her closer, just because he liked her there.

He ended the kiss and set her away from him. He could tell by the look on her dazed face that he had confused her. What was wrong with him? He'd taken a chaste thank-you kiss and turned it into something carnal. Hellfire, it was because he wanted her with everything he had and was.

But he could not have her. Shite, he needed to remember that.

The sound of a lad rustling down the passageway interrupted them.

"Sorry, but Lady Lily is wanted back in the castle. Both chiefs wish to see her."

Lily's face dropped as she handed Sunshine the apple. The horse bit into it, chomping on her treat, and Lily turned to Kyle with a crestfallen face. "Now what have I done?"

Hell, but people had to stop crushing his sweet one's spirits, himself included.

CHAPTER THREE

Lily stepped into the solar where her sire Quade, her stepmother Brenna, and her brother Torrian sat waiting for her. Her shoulders sagged as she moved over to the empty chair and flopped into it, making a major event of straightening her skirts.

Her sire said, "Lily, you know we love you and we're concerned about you."

"There is naught to worry about," she said immediately. "I am fine." She twisted her skirts in her hands, unable to fully concentrate on the present moment because a lad with long dark hair was monopolizing her thoughts. Or was it the kiss she could not get out of her mind? She licked her lips, hoping to savor the taste of him. She stared at the sword hanging on the wall behind her father, her mind lost in the wonderful memory of Kyle.

"Lily? I need you to listen to me," her sire barked.

Oh, he must have said something while she was lost in thought. She gave her father her best smile, pushing Kyle to the back of her mind. How she loved her papa.

"'Tis plain as day to all of us that you feel a bit lost now that Torrian has taken over as chieftain and his wife has assumed your duties."

"What? Where do you get such an addled idea?" She prayed to be forgiven for her lies.

"Lily," Torrian added. "You know naught has changed between you and me, and Heather was only trying to help out by taking over those jobs. She wishes to contribute as the new mistress of the castle."

"You said you were pleased about her taking over your duties," Brenna added.

"I know, Mama. I am pleased, and you know I adore my newest sister." While Torrian had reverted to calling their stepmother by her given name, Lily had not. She was the only mother she'd ever known, and Brenna would always be Mama to her.

Brenna moved her chair closer to Lily's and took hold of her hands. "I think you need to find another interest. Would you like to travel with me in my healer's tasks? On occasion, I could use an extra set of hands."

She gave this careful consideration, for she did enjoy visiting her clanmates, especially the wee ones. "I could help with some," she finally said, "but you know I do not deal well with lots of blood. Bethia and wee Jennet are a better fit for your work." Bethia and Jennet were the healers, not Lily. Jennet was the youngest of the family, but had the quickest mind of all. She loved spending all her time with Mama, working in surgery or as a healer. Much as she'd wanted to, Brenna had not started taking Jennet along for births yet. She'd informed her she was too young, to Jennet's dismay.

"Why do you not take up the bow and arrow with your cousins?" Quade said. "Sorcha, Maggie, and Molly go out every day to practice. They'd be glad to teach you."

"Oh, Papa. I could never hunt an animal, nor watch my cousins kill one. 'Tis not for me."

"But it would mean you could join our annual competitions with the Grants."

"I'll give that some thought." She had absolutely no interest in firing arrows. It was totally out of the realm of possibility for her to ever purposefully injure an animal, and what did she care if an arrow hit a target?

Neither of her parents' suggestions was agreeable to her, but she said, "Of course, I'd be happy to try your suggestions. Please do let me know, Mama, when you think I could be of assistance to you." She nodded her head as if the gesture would convince her family of her sincerity. "May I take my leave now that this problem has been solved?" How many lies was this? She would have to do penance for certes.

Torrian's brow furrowed as he considered his sister. "Och, I know your ways, sister. Naught is solved yet, but I'll allow you to think that it has been. You may try these two tasks, but I do not think either will suit you."

Lily glanced at her beloved brother, trying her best to frown at him—he was right, but she did not wish for her parents to know it—but she could not. She loved Torrian too much to be upset with him. "Torrian, have I told you what a fine job you're doing as our new chieftain?"

"Aye, you have, Lily, and I appreciate it, but I recognize your attempt to distract me. We are still discussing you."

Oh, fiddle. Why did he know her so well?

"Tell us about the man you encountered in the meadow. Why have you not mentioned it to any of us? Kyle told us."

Kyle, the snitch, she'd asked him to stay silent. Now she was in trouble for sure. "When I was in the forest, I heard some rustling behind me. I thought 'twas an animal, but I saw naught. But as it grew closer, I became frightened. I ran back to where I'd entered the forest, and that's when I discovered my dear horse was gone." She stared at her hands, wishing this conversation was over.

Quade said, "Lily, how many times have you been told that the chieftain's daughter does not wander off alone?

Her voice took on a strange tone, almost a shout. "But I'm no longer the chieftain's daughter." She started, surprised at her own vehemence. Judging from the expressions of the three people gathered in front of her, they'd noticed the same edge to her voice. "Forgive me, but I am now the chieftain's sister, as I must remind you."

Quade began to say something, but Lily's mama reached over and tucked his hand in hers, stopping his next sentence short.

"Did you get a good look at this man?" Brenna asked.

Tears misted in her eyes because every answer she gave them made her sound dafter, if that were indeed possible at this point. "Nay, he was dressed in armor. I could not see beneath his helm." She turned her gaze away so she would not have to meet her sire's gaze. She was afraid he would think she had created this story, which would break her heart for sure.

"What color was his hair?" Torrian asked.

"I do believe 'twas brown hair, but mayhap I'm not sure." She stared at her hands in her lap. "He was too far away."

Quade peered at Torrian. "Did anyone check the area?"

"Aye," Torrian responded. "Kyle checked the area after he

brought Lily back, and while there was evidence of trampled grass…"

"You see? I am not daft. Kyle saw." Lily leaned forward in her chair, hoping this was enough for them to believe her.

"…it could have been from our own men hunting. 'Tis a favorite area."

Quade said, "I want another slew of guards checking the area again today. You send them in all four directions. I need to know who was on our land."

Lily did her best not to pay much attention to them since she knew they were not worried about her. Torrian and her father were always so logical and forthright, the exact opposite of her. She could not help but wonder if her mother, Lilias, had been more like Lily—light of heart. After all, she must have gotten it from somewhere. She shared absolutely naught in common with her sire and her brother. She snorted.

From the way her sire and brother stared at her, she'd done so loud enough for all to hear. She smiled at her sire, not wanting to explain herself, and folded her hands back in her lap.

A light rap sounded at the door just then, and Torrian barked, "Enter."

One of the maids entered and said, "Forgive me, my lairds, but Lady Brenna has been requested at Mary's cottage. A healer is needed."

Brenna stood immediately. "Tell them we'll be right along."

We? Could that word mean what Lily thought it meant? She did not have to wonder for long. The maid left quickly, and Brenna turned to face Lily. "Are you ready?"

Lily started. "For what, Mama?"

"Well, this is a birthing. I could use your assistance, if you are free. Bethia is not feeling well today. You know she loves to assist, but I would prefer she stay back."

What a silly comment. Of course, she was free. Did she wish to go? Nay.

"Of course, Mama, I would love to attend the birthing with you." It was lie number…goodness, how was she to keep track of all her terrible lies? She thought it had been less than five, but she had to admit she didn't know.

Lily followed her mama out the door of the solar, and Lady

Brenna accepted her healer's satchel from the maid before heading out the door of the great hall. "Now, daughter," she said, glancing back at Lily, "you do not need to watch the birth if the blood bothers you. You may help with gathering towels, heating water, or consoling sweet Mary as she delivers this bairn. She has three others that you could care for while we're busy. Whatever you wish to do is acceptable to me."

Goodness, but she was learning the problem with lying. She had no desire to attend a birthing. All that blood and screaming... She'd be sure to faint to the floor.

As she trailed behind her mother, she smiled at all the clanspeople who were moving aside for Lady Brenna. They knew how important her work was whenever she carried her satchel. Lily wondered if they'd ever show her that same respect. Nay, they preferred to stop and stare at Lily, acting as if she had two heads attached to her shoulder. She giggled at the image that popped into her head.

Her mama gave her a strange look, but continued to make haste toward the cabin. "You'll find your own way, lass," she said, still moving quickly as she spoke. "I'm sure of it. You are a talented and loveable young woman."

"Mama, are you any good at catching things?" Lily rubbed her head. The more she thought about it, the more certain she was she would faint during the delivery. How she hoped her dear stepmother would be able to catch her before she cracked her head open on the stone floor.

"Whatever do you mean, Lily?" Brenna gave her a perplexed look, but there was no time to explain. They'd reached Mary's cottage, and the lass's sire was standing in front of the door, wide-eyed. "Please help her. And if you can..." he whispered. "Can you not help her husband, as well? The man is quite addled with this one."

Lily and Brenna stepped into the cottage. Lily's first reaction was to cover her ears. Everyone was screaming. Brenna moved straight into the adjoining chamber, the source of the loudest screams, to attend to Mary, but Lily stayed put in the front of the cottage. A large man wearing a beleaguered expression on his face sat in the corner with a screaming child on his lap, a lass around one summer old. Two other lassies sat on the floor crying, though

Lily had no idea why. She glanced at the man, who said, "Help me, please? I know not what to do without my Mary. The bairn is hungry and she cannot feed her."

Lily headed over to the table near the hearth and searched through the food baskets until she found a carrot and a hunk of bread. She took the wee lassie from her sire's arms and sat on a stool near the hearth on the opposite wall. The father, clearly grateful, stood and said, "My apologies, but they've been like this since Mary started with the baby last night. I just need a moment, lass. Please?" When she nodded her answer, he slipped out the door.

Lily settled the bairn on her lap, placed the carrot in the wean's mouth so she had something to gnaw on, and waved the other crying girls over to a spot beside her. All three bairns were still crying, but the wee one stopped every so often to gnaw on the carrot for a few seconds. Unsure of how she could calm them, she did the only thing she could think of to help maintain her own sanity.

Lily began to sing. She started off by humming, but once the two bairns on the floor started to listen—their tears turned to mere sniffles—she sang with all her heart, about her horse and rainbows and flowers and all the things dear to her. The singing carried her away, and she almost missed it when the lassies on the floor leaned over and snuggled together, one of them placing her thumb in her mouth. None of the bairns were even sniffling now.

Pleased with her small success, Lily continued, singing even louder. Eventually, the older lassies curled up on the floor and closed their eyes. Within moments, they were asleep as fast as slumbering newborns. The wee lass in Lily's arms continued to gnaw on the carrot, her mouth turning orange, her wee gaze locked on Lily's mouth as she continued to sing. Eventually the wean pulled the carrot from her mouth and closed her eyes, letting her head rest in the crook of Lily's arms.

Once the three girls' bellowing had stopped, Lily noticed Mary was no longer screaming either. Not daring to stop her singing because it was so peaceful, she continued until the door to the inner chamber opened. Her mama stood there holding a squealing bairn, though the child's cries couldn't come even close to the screaming that had come from the other three. Brenna carried the child over closer to Lily, motioning for her to continue her song, and the child stopped its squealing, closed its eyes, and nestled into Brenna's arms.

At the sound of the babe, the front door flew open and Mary's husband reappeared. His gaze fell on Lily first, and Mary's sire, who had entered behind him, stared at Lily as well. Though the attention discomfited her, she continued with her song, afraid the bairns would all awaken screaming if she stopped.

Mary's husband then turned to stare at Brenna. "My lady?"

"Congratulations, Sorley. Your wife has gifted you with a son." She held the lad up to Sorley, and the man fell onto a stool. Tears erupted from his eyes as he staggered up and took his son from her, then ran into the chamber. "Mary, we have a son. Finally, a wee laddie."

Brenna moved over to close the door, giving the couple some privacy with their new babe, and then turned to Lily. "Well done. I've never seen anyone quiet bairns the way you did." Brenna found a plaid on a chair and tucked it around the two lassies snuggled together sound asleep on the floor. She then took the sleeping bairn from Lily's arm and settled her into the swaddled drawer in a nearby chest.

Mary's sire glanced at Lily and said, "Bless you, lassie. You are a true gift from God."

He settled in a chair by the hearth, letting out a deep sigh as he leaned back and closed his eyes.

Lily had no idea how the man could consider her a gift from God.

He wouldn't say so if he knew all the lies she'd told.

CHAPTER FOUR

Kyle stood in the doorway to the laird's chamber, his palms sweating and his heart racing. Why had they called him in? Had he done something wrong? Would they fire him because he had failed in his duty to take care of Lily? Aye, he should have guessed she'd leave the castle grounds on her own again. She'd been too unsettled lately, too unpredictable. He'd have to talk to her again about being more careful.

As soon as Quade and Torrian ended their conversation and gave him their attention, he cleared his throat and said, "My lairds. You requested my presence?"

Quade stood and limped to Kyle's side. "Aye, I did, Kyle. For three reasons. First I'd like to congratulate you on a job well done. You've done a fine job as Torrian's second. You're a hardworking lad, and I know your sire would be proud of you. I wish he were here to share in your success."

"Many thanks, my laird." Even though Torrian was the official laird now, Kyle continued to call Quade by the same title out of respect. He was not alone in this. "I wish my sire were here, as well. I know my mother misses him as much as I do." Kyle's father had died from an injury incurred during the battle to save Avelina Ramsay, Quade's sister, many years ago.

"My apologies my wife was not able to save him." Quade moved back to his seat. "Sit, lad. You work hard enough all day."

Kyle recalled how hard Lady Brenna had worked to save his sire, going so far as to bring him into the keep to tend his wounds. His sire had received a sword wound to the leg that should not have been serious, but he hadn't tended to it right away as Lady Brenna always advised. It had festered on the road back home, and she'd been unable to stop it from taking his life. Whatever it was that caused wounds to slowly kill strong men, even small nicks, he hoped Lady Brenna would be able to figure it out. If any healer could do it, she was the one.

Even though the loss was an old one, Kyle still missed his sire every day of his life. And he did aught he could to make his father proud. He could not jeopardize his position as Torrian's second.

Kyle sat in the proffered chair. "Many thanks, my laird."

"Now, the second reason I asked you here is to find out what you learned of this supposed attack on my daughter. You need not tell me how foolish she was to go out on her own. She's been chastised enough by me and her stepmother, but I'd like to hear what you found when you came upon her."

Kyle nodded, organizing his thoughts carefully before he spoke. "When I noticed she was missing, I headed to the gates. The guards told me she'd left for a brief ride, but the thought of waiting for her return did not sit well, so I headed out across the meadow. Once I reached the halfway point, I could hear a lass screaming. I saw Lily tearing across the meadow as if she was being chased by a wild animal, but I did not notice any pursuers, only a rider on horseback heading away from the forest. I did not recognize him, and since he was moving away, I did not concern myself with him. Mayhap 'twas a mistake. When I approached her, she was so frightened she had trouble telling me what had transpired. She finally explained that a man in chain mail and a helm had chased her, asking for her to stop and declaring that he loved her. I checked the area later, but found naught out of the ordinary, just some trampled grass in the forest."

Quade glanced at Torrian. "She did not mention to me that the attacker had declared his love for her. Did she mention this to you, Torrian?"

"Nay. Other than that, her story was the same."

"Was there aught else out of the ordinary?" Quade asked Kyle.

"Only that Sunshine had run off. Lily had left her to graze outside the forest, and when she returned, the horse was nowhere to be seen."

"Hmmm. She rarely needs to tether Sunshine." Quade rubbed his knee as he considered this new information.

"Nay. Sunshine always stays by her side," Torrian agreed.

"Kyle, many thanks for doing your job and finding her, but I must ask you a serious question. Please consider your answer for a moment before you give it." Quade paused, waiting for a response from him.

Kyle nodded, but his mind raced with panic. What in hell was Quade about to ask him?

"Do you believe 'tis possible that Lily created the entire incident to draw attention to herself?" Quade leaned back in his chair while he waited for Kyle's answer.

"What? You think Lily made it up?"

"Nay, I did not say that. I'm asking you if you think 'tis possible. It concerns me how unsettled Lily has been since Torrian's marriage. I had hoped it would be a passing stage, but she has not returned to herself. I'd like to hear your thoughts on this since you were the one who found her."

Kyle could not imagine his Lily lying about something so serious. He knew her well, hell, he *loved* her. "Nay, my laird. Lily did not make the tale up. I saw a genuinely frightened lass when I came upon her. And I might add that she would never have chased off Sunshine to back up her tale. You know how she adores that horse. It took me half the night to find Sunshine, so the danger to her was real."

"Good point," Torrian said with a nod. "Da, he's correct in that assessment. She would not have risked Sunshine for a fabrication. I have to agree with him."

Quade considered their answers, rubbing his chin in thought. "Mayhap you are correct."

Silence settled between them, broken only when Torrian cleared his throat and stared at his sire. Kyle thought that did not bode well for him. His best friend did not wish to look him in the eye.

"All right," Quade said. "That pleases me. I'd hate to believe that of my Lily. I have already given Torrian instructions to search the area. In view of what you've just told me, I'd like a score of guards to troll the periphery of our land every day until we determine who that was. The rider frightened Lily, and he was not of our clan. I wish to know who he is."

"I will see to it, my laird." Kyle said.

"And please keep a careful eye on Lily. I know you always do, but she is unsettled ever since Torrian married Heather." He glanced at Torrian and at Kyle to ensure his point was made to both. Kyle nodded his affirmation that he would indeed continue to protect her. "Kyle, my thanks that you were as observant as you were about our Lily. You know how much she means to all of us."

Kyle stared at the ground. *If he only knew how much she meant to him.*

"That brings me to the final reason I asked you here."

"Aye, my laird?" A new moistness flooded his palms as he waited. Would he be fired? Sent away? What ill news awaited him?

"Have I noticed something building between you and Lily?"

Kyle opened his mouth to deny it, but Quade held his hand up to stop him. "Please. Allow me to rephrase this. Brenna and I believe 'tis time for our daughter to consider marriage. So I'd like to ask you before anyone else. Would you consider a betrothal to Lily?"

If a frog had hopped across in front of him at that very moment, the slight breeze would have felled Kyle. His mind seemed to explode with a hundred thoughts at once. He had no idea how to answer that question. None at all.

Torrian said, "Kyle? Are you well? You look a wee bit green."

Kyle stared at his friend and nodded. His dream had just been handed to him. He'd always wished to marry Lily and thought about how sweet life would be if he could love her, cherish her, take care of her. But he was new to his position, and besides, he needed to take care of his mother. If he were married to Lily, he'd never be able to do his duty to his clan and his sire. Why, he'd been so distracted by her this morning, he'd almost cut off his own hand.

He glanced at Torrian in mute shock. If he wedded Lily, he'd be related to his best friend. The thought had never before occurred to him.

"Kyle?" Quade asked, glancing from Quade to Kyle.

Would Lily even have him? She'd been furious with him earlier—she'd actually thrown dirt at him. But she had also kissed him. Mayhap they should talk first.

"Have you asked Lily?" Kyle managed to get out.

"Nay, I'm asking you first. Your response?" Quade drummed his fingers on the arm of his chair.

"I am well. I…I…I do not know what to say. Lily is a beautiful young lass, but I…if we were to…how could I? I do not know how I could take care of a wife while doing my duty as Torrian's second. Besides," he rushed on, "I am sure Lily is not interested in me at all. She may not have mentioned it, but we often argue. We probably would not suit. We…"

Quade held his hand up. "You've answered my question. I see you are not ready for married life yet. Please do not mention this to Lily. I thought I saw something there that does not exist. Forgive me if I have upset you, lad. In fact, you may go."

Kyle stood up so fast, he was light-headed. "Many thanks, my lairds." He nodded to both Quade and Torrian and rushed out of the room, across the courtyard, and through the gates until he was outside the castle. Only then did he expel the breath he'd been holding.

Betrothed to Lily? He wanted naught more than to be betrothed to Lily. But how could he wed her without failing in his duties and disgracing his sire? Mayhap it would help if they waited a year or more, until he was more steadfast in his job? Would Lily be willing to have a long betrothal?

He ran his hand through his hair, wishing to slap himself. It was too late to ask that question now.

And besides, he had to make a choice. When it came down to it, he could either satisfy himself by marrying Lily or he could continue doing aught he could to make his sire proud and take care of his mother.

Responsibility had always guided Kyle's actions, so his answer was obvious.

Lily spoke in a quiet soothing tone to her horse as she rubbed her down. "Sunshine, how will I ever get this dirt from your white coat? You must have rolled on the ground, did you not?"

Sunshine whinnied and lifted her head as if to nod to Lily.

"I missed you too, Sunshine. What would I ever do without you? I was so frightened when you were missing. He was a bad man, a verra bad man. I'm forever grateful you are safe."

Sunshine nudged her.

"Aye, I know you like Kyle. I think you flirt with him. He is the only one who could bring you home. Or possibly Torrian."

Sunshine was still in the special room in the stables, but Lily thought to take her outside today. First she had to make sure Kyle was not around, or else he'd shout at her again.

She hadn't seen Kyle in two days. After her adventure with her mama and the babies, she'd stayed hidden all day yesterday, but she had needed some space and air, so she'd headed straight for her sweet mare.

"Sunshine, you are my only true friend, but I believe you know that, do you not?"

The horse snorted and pushed against Lily's hand, looking for her love. She rubbed the soft fur of the horse's neck, only for her fingers to be caught once again by the mess in her mane. "Sunshine, much as I hate to do this to you, your ribbons are frayed and your mane is a mess. I can no longer allow you to look so bedraggled. I must make you beautiful once more."

Lily reached for the ribbons and carefully pulled each one out, tending to the fine hairs of her mare's white mane as she worked. Sunshine always allowed Lily's ministrations, whatever they were. After a little while, she decided to fetch a better brushing tool.

"Sunshine, I must make you forever beautiful, so forgive me for leaving you for a few moments. I must fetch the better curry-comb."

She took off down the corridor. The Ramsay stables had grown so large that one could be at the far end without knowing who else was inside. Sound did not carry well because of the number of horses that were kept there. Quade was forever adding new stalls so his favorite horses could be kept inside for much of the winter. She reached the storage supply chamber and ducked inside, pleased to find it empty.

As she searched for the proper comb, though, she heard Aunt Gwyneth and Uncle Logan's voices from the stall next to her. Not normally one to eavesdrop, she could not help but overhear a comment that caused her to freeze in place.

"Logan, I know she's your dearest niece, but you must allow her to grow up on her own."

Dearest niece? Were they talking about her? She could not walk away until she knew for certes, so she stayed.

"Gwynie, I cannot stand by and allow the two of them to make such a big mistake. How could the lad be so foolish? There is not another lad on Ramsay land or in any of the surrounding clans who would turn down the opportunity to be betrothed to Lily. What the hellfire is wrong with him?"

Lily's eyes, which now felt as big as the saddles hung on the nearby wall, darted around the chamber as if to find something hiding. Could she have heard them correctly? She tiptoed as quietly as possible over to the wall. She had to hear every word of their conversation.

"I think you need to give them both time. They're both young, and Kyle has just been promoted to this new position. Lads focus on their fighting skills first. You know he's smitten with her, he is simply not ready."

Still uncertain as to what they discussed, she could not deny that her heart just skipped a beat or two to hear her aunt say that Kyle was smitten with her. Was he? Naught would make her happier than to be sure of his love.

"Nay, a lad who was truly smitten would not turn down such a request from his laird. I may have to have a wee talk with the lad. They were meant for each other. Why can they not see it?"

"I agree with you, but they must come to this on their own, and you need to stay out of the matter."

There was the sound of movement, a stall door opening and closing, and then Torrian's voice burst out in the adjoining stall. "Good morn to you all. I see Molly, Maggie, and Sorcha await you outside."

Lily crept back down to Sunshine's stall, afraid her brother would sense her close presence. She fought the tears that threatened to spill down her cheeks, drench the front of her, and land in a huge puddle beneath her.

So her papa had suggested a betrothal to Kyle and Kyle had refused.

Saints above, she had worried Kyle did not return her feelings, and here was the proof. Smitten. Apparently he was far from smitten. "Sunshine, did you hear that? Without conferring with me, my father asked Kyle if he wanted to marry me. Kyle refused." She wrapped her arms around her beloved horse's neck as the tears continued to track down her cheeks. Sunshine snorted and pawed the ground, but Lily could not stop.

Tears blurred her vision terribly, but she stood up straight, intent on finishing her chore. She pulled the braids out of the horse's mane and combed through her fine white hair. Sunshine snorted again, and Lily responded, "I'm not up to putting more ribbons in your hair just now. You'll just have to go without for a few days."

She said naught as she continued with her task. The white beast did its best to nudge Lily into a better mood, but to no avail. Lily cried until she had no more tears. "I hate him, I hate everything about him. I'll never speak a word to that lad again."

Silence settled on her again until she whispered, "I know, Sunshine. I've told another lie. Do not worry, I am counting. I'll apologize to my dearest Lord when I'm sure I've finished lying."

She sniffled a few more times before she made an announcement. "In fact, I think I'll change your name from Sunshine to Tilly."

Her aunt Gwyneth, an able hunter, slipped into the stall before she heard the sound of approaching footsteps.

"Lily?"

Aunt Gwyneth was a woman of few words.

"Good day to you, Auntie." She sniffled and hitched her breath a few times before she could bear to look at her aunt.

"Problems? Aught I can do to help?"

Lily shook her head. "Nay. I'm upset with the number of knots in Tilly's lovely mane. But I've managed to remove most of them."

"Tilly? Is that not Sunshine?"

"Mayhap." Lily's breath hitched three more times before she could speak. "I've changed her name to Tilly. It suits her better."

"Aye, she is your horse to name as you choose. Would you like to go shooting arrows with Sorcha, Molly, Maggie, and me?"

Lily's first instinct was to refuse, but then an unbidden thought changed her answer. "Aye, I'll go, but you'll have to teach me again, Aunt Gwyneth."

"I'd be happy to. I did not think you'd accept."

Lily stopped her sniveling, lifted her chin a notch, and replied. "I was planning to refuse, but I've changed my mind."

"Good. Whatever changed your mind, it pleases me. We'll await you outside."

After Gwyneth left, she leaned over to whisper to her horse.

"Tilly, you must come with me. I need to learn how to fire an arrow into Kyle Maule's arse."

CHAPTER FIVE

Kyle headed out to visit his mother. As Torrian's second, he slept with the guards in their building, but he still checked on his mother often. He passed Seamus on the way, and the older man gave him a brief update on the search. "We have not found aught more than the tracks we discovered on the first day, Kyle. The man who followed Lily has left, probably chased away by the guards we've had combing the area. I'm convinced he's taken his leave, at least for now."

"Stay diligent, Seamus."

"Aye, our men are out there. We'll not let aught happen to our Lily." He nodded and moved past Kyle.

Kyle simply nodded. Seamus was one of the best. He and Mungo had acted interchangeably as Quade's second, and they had both agreed to stay on to assist Kyle in his new role. He trusted them implicitly, but his mind was elsewhere. Two days had passed since his meeting in the laird's solar, and he couldn't get past the feeling that he'd made the biggest mistake of his life. Ironically, while he'd done what he thought he needed to do in order to stay focused on his job as Torrian's second, he was more distracted than ever. Lily, sweet Lily, was a distraction to him no matter what. He loved her with all his heart, and he did *not* wish to live his life without her. Unfortunately, he hadn't come up with a solution.

His mother still lived in the same small cottage where he'd grown up. The hut was a distance from the bailey. His mother kept it spotless, and there were neighbors in the area, but Kyle wished she were closer since she was now alone. The stone walls held up well, and the thatched roof had barely any water leaks, but his sire had always been meticulous about providing for his mother.

Kyle needed to continue to do the same.

He finally reached his mother's cottage. Part of him wished to confide in her, but he could not bear to tell her he'd refused his laird's offer of a betrothal to Lily.

"Kyle? What's wrong? Are you not feeling well?" His mother kneaded her hands in her skirt, a habit of hers.

"Nay, I'm fine, Mama." Hell, he was far from fine. Sick would be the proper word. It made him sick to think he'd just made the biggest mistake of his life. "Mama, I told our laird that if a cottage ever became available inside the bailey, I'd like you to move into it."

His mother frowned. "Kyle, nay. I do not wish to move. I like it here." Her gaze scanned the room at all the things she'd done to make it warm and comfortable. Kyle knew the feel of every soft cushion, warm plaid, and the smell of her soaps and her carefully kneaded breads.

Kyle was an only child, so he was the only one around to care for his mother. "But Mama, you would be much safer inside the bailey. And you are getting on in age…"

"Kyle Maule, do not insult your mother so. I know I am older than *you*, but I have quite a bit of life left in me. I'd prefer to live out my remaining years here in my home."

He'd expected she would balk at moving, particularly since the cottage held the sweet memories of his sire, but he was concerned about his mother's safety. Well, he'd done as planned. Mayhap she would see the wisdom of his words in time.

It was probably best that she hadn't agreed to move yet, anyway. After refusing the betrothal to Lily, he doubted that either of his lairds would be willing to give him a boon for aught. He'd just have to continue to work hard and hope a cottage became available.

"Kyle, you love her, do you not?"

His mother's whispered words took him by surprise. "What?"

"Lily. You love her. You always have."

"How did you know?"

"Mothers know these things. Why do you not ask to court her? Our beloved Lily has grown up, and she will marry. Do not miss your chance."

"Mama, I must focus on being the best possible second to our laird…and taking good care of you just as Da did."

"Kyle, I appreciate all you do for me, but I am capable of taking care of most everything on my own. For certes, I do not want you to postpone marriage because you think you need to care for me. I would love to gain a daughter." Her smile told him she was speaking in earnest. So many days had been heartbreaking for her after the loss of his sire. He was pleased to see she had finally adjusted to life without his father.

"I'll think on it, Mama, but I cannot overlook my responsibilities. You know I wish to make Da proud."

"You *have* made him proud. Being assigned the laird's second would have made your sire prouder than aught."

Indecision still weighed heavy on Kyle's shoulders. "Do you not know the pressure I feel to perform my assignment well?"

Kyle's mother rushed over to wrap her arm over his shoulders. "Aye, 'tis true, Kyle. I believe you must focus for now. Just remember that it does not mean you should never marry."

"Seamus never married. He said he could not do both. Mayhap I am the same."

"Nay, I think not. I'd prefer to see you happy in your life outside your responsibilities. Think on it, please?"

"Aye, I will." He knew it was a promise he would carry out, for he could not stop thinking about Lily. Why, he'd been enchanted with the wee lass from the first moment he met her. Kyle turned away from his mother and stared out the window, his mind focused on a memory from long ago when he was ten summers and Lily was around five.

Kyle's mother and father had brought him to the keep to visit with Torrian. The clan had long believed the laird's son was dead, so it had been a shock to all of them to discover he was not only alive, but *healed* and living in the great hall. The laird himself had requested Kyle's presence that day, and his parents had been anxious to bring him along. Kyle was enchanted by the opportunity to visit the great hall and spend time with the laird's family. He'd heard of Torrian and his sister, Lily, but he'd never had the chance to talk with either of them.

"Torrian has been sick for many years," his mother said as they approached the keep, "but he has healed thanks to the laird's new wife, Brenna. Now Torrian needs to have some friends, and our laird has honored your father by asking him to bring you to visit with him. Now please be a good laddie and be polite."

Kyle was so awestruck by the close-up view of the huge keep that he did not say a word. Even the door was bigger than his father. His parents ushered him inside, and before he knew it, he was sitting across from Torrian at a table near the hearth, and his mama and da were strolling around the room with the laird and his new wife.

Torrian reached down to pet the head of the giant Deerhound at his feet. He was a thin boy with fair hair, but not as light as Lily's. Though he was not standing, Kyle guessed him to be taller than he was, and he sat straight as an arrow in his chair. He noticed the soft cushions on Torrian's chair, wondered if he was well yet. He did not think on it again because Torrian's mind was sharp as any he'd ever encountered.

"Greetings," Kyle said, just as his mother had instructed him to do.

"Greetings to you. What is your name?"

"Kyle. What is...? Och, never mind. I do know, you're Torrian."

"My parents made you come, did they not?"

Kyle thought it would not sound nice to agree, so he hesitated before answering. "Aye, but I wanted to come."

"Why?" Torrian asked.

"To see what it was like inside. I've never been here before." His gaze took in the high-beamed ceiling, the tapestries on the wall, the fresh rushes on the floor, and the wee lass darting around the room like a wee elf made of golden curls and giggles. "Who's that?"

"That's my sister, Lily."

"I've never seen her before." He guessed her to be around five summers, though he couldn't tell for sure.

"Trust me, you will. She'll come closer. She moves everywhere."

"What are you playing?" Kyle said, taking in the board set out before the other boy.

"Chess. Do you know how to play?"

Kyle shook his head.

"Would you like to learn? I'll teach you."

"Aye."

And he did. Kyle soaked up Torrian's every word as he tried to remember the rules of the game. Then Lily interrupted them by racing over to Kyle's side of the table.

"Torrian, who is your new friend?" she asked, planting her hands on the bench next to Kyle and staring straight at him. "Did you see how fast I am?" she asked.

"This is Kyle, Lily. Please do not bother him over much, I'm trying to teach him how to play chess."

"All right, but I must do two things first."

"Go ahead. I know you'll not stop until I give in." Torrian gave Kyle an apologetic look.

Lily giggled and said, "I love you, Torrian. You're my favorite of all. Watch me run, Kyle. See if I'm not the fastest person you've ever seen."

Kyle turned his face back to Torrian to see what Torrian thought of her request, but the wee one refused to be ignored. She climbed up on the bench, leaned toward him, and placed her tiny hand on his cheek, forcing him to look at her. "You cannot see me run if you look at my brother. You must watch me. My, but you have the bluest eyes I've ever seen, Kyle."

Kyle nodded and gave her his full attention, watching as she took off around the chamber, darting around trestle tables as she giggled and tossed her golden locks this way and that. Finally, she stopped in front of him, panting and leaning toward him. He was so fascinated with her antics—he'd never seen someone with so much energy—that he'd turned around on the bench to watch her without realizing what he was doing.

Her eyes danced and sparkled, and she had a smile on her face the likes of which he'd never seen before. "Am I not the fastest of all, Kyle?" She hopped up and down while she waited for his response.

Her smile never dissipated, and Kyle recalled his father's admonishment to be polite to all of the Ramsays. He decided telling a lie to a wee one was not so bad. "Aye, you are the fastest one here, Lily."

"Oh! I knew it!" She laughed and jumped up and down,

clapping her wee hands together before she leaned toward him and wrapped her arms around him in a tight squeeze.

"Why'd you do that?" Kyle asked, puzzled by the strange gesture.

"You do not know? Why, 'twas a hug! Do you not know what a hug is?" Her eyes widened, and she stepped back, but the smile still did not leave her face.

He shook his head. Aye, his mother had kissed him on the cheek, and he'd seen his father embrace his mother, but he did not recall ever being embraced by a lass in such a way.

"Then you must have another." She reached for him and hugged him again, yellow strands of her hair drifting into his face along with a sweet aroma of flowers.

Still puzzled, he said naught, but he let her have her way. He would never forget what she said next.

"Did you not know, Kyle? A hug makes everything better. Do you not agree?" With that, she laughed again and ran off.

"Sorry about my sister," Torrian said. "Some lads find her annoying."

Kyle, his gaze still following the enchanting lass around the hall, had answered, "Not me. I like her."

He'd never made a truer statement in his life.

That was the beginning of a wonderful friendship between Kyle and Torrian.

Kyle stared out of the window, his mind still focused on Lily. She'd flown into his life as if on the wings of an angel, and thankfully, she'd never left. Each day Lily's essence had dug a wee bit deeper into his soul until the initial liking he'd felt had turned to a love that frightened him.

"Mama, I have a new position that carries much responsibility," he finally muttered, realizing he had stayed silent too long. "I cannot involve myself with such frivolous things. You know how I wish to make Da proud."

"Oh, Kyle." She moved over to place her hand on her son's shoulder. "Love is not frivolous. 'Tis as necessary for a lad as it is for a lass. Someday you'll see. You and Lily were meant for each other. Even your da would wish for you to marry. Why can you not see that?"

"Mama?" He leaned down to kiss her cheek. "I must go. Send someone to fetch me if you need aught."

And he headed out the door. Under no circumstances could he discuss his love for Lily with his mother. It was just too painful.

Lily followed her aunt and cousins out to the archery field on Tilly's back. Once outside the stables, her smile returned. The day was so glorious, how could she not smile? She'd force herself to forget that bothersome Kyle and enjoy herself. The sun shone, just as her Sunshine...or Tilly did.

Once they reached the field, Lily hopped down and ran over to join her aunt at the archery chest, which was kept stocked at all times for anyone who wished to practice. As soon as she opened the chest, Lily's gaze shot to one thing inside—ribbons. "Auntie, where did you find all those beautiful ribbons?"

"I use them on my arrows sometimes. It helps me to see at a distance which one is which. Logan purchased them for me at the fair in Edinburgh. Do you like them?"

Lily's hand caressed the deep blue velvet ribbon on top. "Aye, 'tis most lovely."

"Lily, you may take them out if you'd like." Gwyneth patted her hand.

"May I? My thanks." She could not help herself. She tugged out a few pink ribbons and yellow ones to see which she liked best. Why, the pink would look lovely on Sun...Tilly's mane. She could braid it in while she was out here. She glanced at her horse, but the mare was grazing in the field, content, so she put the ribbons back for later.

She reminded herself of her purpose. It was time for her to learn how to hit a target right in the middle. Kyle's muscled bottom came to mind, and she smiled, but then frowned at the image of her arrow bouncing off his tight muscle. Hmmm...she'd have to take a peek at his breeches under his plaid the next time she saw him. She could not recall if he was muscular there or not.

Then she recalled how her cousin Jennie had first met the man she married by hitting him in the arse with her arrow. Apparently, Jennie couldn't shoot her bow any better than Lily did. Mayhap this could be a good plan. She stared into the sky imagining Kyle's reaction to Lily hitting his arse with her arrow. Just the thought of it sent her into a fit of giggles.

"Who is the lad you're dreaming of?" Sorcha asked, elbowing Lily from the side.

"Cousin, I know not of what you speak. I was doing no such thing. Why, if I were to dream of any lad, it would be of hitting them in the arse with an arrow."

"Lily!" Maggie barked. "I've never heard you speak in such a way."

Molly giggled and said, "But I like the new you."

The four cousins laughed together while Gwyneth set up three targets in a row. Once she was finished, she gave each of them a bow and lined them up, starting with her daughters, before moving on to Lily. "All right, Lily. Show me what you recall from your last lesson."

Trying to remember all she'd been taught, Lily lined herself up with the target, nocked her arrow, and let it loose. She heard a large thwack and hopped up and down. "I hit something, I did it, Aunt Gwyneth, I actually hit the target!"

Sorcha laughed so hard she was holding her middle, her finger extended and pointing toward the targets. Molly and Maggie glanced at the targets and covered their giggles the best they could. Glowering at them, Lily asked, "Why are you laughing so hard?"

Gwyneth took her niece's chin and forced her to look at the targets. Lily's face fell.

"You hit Sorcha's target, not yours." Gwyneth rubbed her shoulder to comfort her.

Lily laughed along with others, but she felt crushed on the inside. Why could she never measure up? Gwyneth's daughters were so talented in everything they did. She was useless at so many things.

"Och, Lily, I swear you're our favorite cousin. We always laugh when you're with us, and you never fail to brighten our day," Molly said.

Lily knew Molly was trying to cheer her up, so she decided to forget about her mistake and move on. "Aunt Gwyneth, I believe I need to brush up on your teachings. Would you mind showing me again?"

Gwyneth winked at her and said, "I'd love to show you again."

Gwyneth worked with her for more than an hour. While she did improve, most of her arrows still flew way out of range. Her shoulders slumped, so Gwyneth said, "Why do you not take a rest for a moment? Your arms are probably fatigued. You can try again in a few minutes."

Thrilled for the reprieve, Lily grabbed the water skin. Once she had refreshed herself, she noticed Gwyneth was now working with Molly, so she decided to stay out of their way. She wandered over to the chest to peek at the ribbons again.

As soon as she opened the top and her gaze fell on all the beautiful colors, her soul thrummed a new song. She had a wonderful idea, so she set herself to her task, weaving and tying the ribbons together until she was pleased with her finished product. That aim accomplished, she stood up and held her face up to the sky, feeling the light breeze against her cheeks, smiling as she noticed her horse trotting toward her. "Why, Tilly? I do believe 'tis the most perfect day."

Enthralled in her new project, she was oblivious to everything except her horse and her ribbons. She'd tied them together and attached them to the end of a long stick, and when she lifted it up, they flowed all the way to the ground and beyond. "Let me know how it looks behind me, Tilly. I'm sure you will love it. This reminds me of your beautiful braids." She hugged her horse and set off across the field.

Her face tipped toward the sun, she launched in the opposite direction of the archery fields, weaving different paths through the meadow, waving the ribbons behind her as she gallivanted about.

"Oh my, Tilly. Look how high the ribbons float behind me. Do you not love these colors?" She hummed for a while before she began to put words to her song, singing about the rain and the animals in the meadows, the mist in the Highlands, and the songs always in her heart. Eventually, she began to twirl and wave the ribbons about. "Look, Tilly," she yelled. "See how the ribbons twirl about me!"

She sang her favorite song, one she'd made up as a wee lass.

Ramsay land is bonny land,
'twill be in my heart forever.
'Tis the land of mountains, glens, and lochs,
And thistles, bluebells, and heather.

She leaped this way and that, giggling between verses as the ribbons floated around her. How magical it felt!

As she completed different turns and leaps, the ribbons drifted about her, sometimes draping over her shoulders, sometimes entwining in her long curls, and sometimes floating through the air as she leaped as high as she could before landing and completing a pirouette.

Out of the corner of her eye, she noticed her cousins had stopped to watch her and were applauding her special leaps. She thought they spoke to her, but she was so enraptured with her song that she couldn't hear them. Spinning and spinning, she laughed until her belly hurt, not paying attention to anyone around her until she saw a cloud of dust headed her way.

CHAPTER SIX

Kyle stared out of his mother's doorway, unable to believe the sight in front of him. The wee minx would be the death of him yet. Lily was with her aunt Gwyneth, a fierce warrior, so she should be safe, but Gwyneth was tending to the archery field while her daughters watched Lily frolic in a far-off meadow.

Kyle's gut clenched as he watched several villagers approach the field, coming in groups to watch Lily sing, sway, and leap through the meadow. True, she was a beautiful sight, her golden waves loosened from her plait and flowing down behind her, her arm lifting a branch high so the ribbons she'd connected to it waved in the wind behind her, but had they no sense?

Lily running free could invite any stranger from the nearby woods to attack her. Had she forgotten about the man who'd followed her before, declaring his love to her? What if he were nearby? She was so far from him that Kyle would never be able to catch up if the stranger hoisted her onto his horse.

The decision was so obvious, it did not even feel like a decision. Kyle raced for his horse and mounted in a second, flicking the reins and spurring his horse straight toward Lily. The more he saw her twirl, the more frightened he became. Plenty of people stood on the edges of the field now, applauding her, encouraging her to continue, but Kyle thought he'd die ten deaths until he got her out of there.

He bellowed the Ramsay whoop to advise the others to clear the way for him. He could tell Lily was still oblivious to him, and he hoped she didn't hit him with that stick, but he had to get to her before anyone else could. Naught would stop him from protecting his Lily.

Kyle rode past his clanspeople, heading to one side of the dancing lass so he could scoop her up with his arm and settle her on the horse with him. He knew he took a chance, but Quade had forced his men to practice such a maneuver in case they ever needed to rescue women or children from danger.

Only in the last few seconds did she finally whirl around to stare at him, dropping her stick with the ribbons in fright as he drew up beside her, reached down to grab her by the waist, and settled her in front of him.

"Kyle Maule," she ground out before he knocked the wind from her. Once she was able to speak again, she said, "What are you doing?"

"What am I doing? What are you doing? Have you no sense? Do you not recall the man who attempted to kidnap you? By running through the middle of the meadow, you've given him an open target. You'll be the death of me yet, lassie. How can I possibly protect the chief's sister when she does not think about her actions?" Hellfire, but his heart had been in his throat until she landed safely in his lap.

"Put me down, Kyle. I was enjoying myself. For once, I managed to forget about this foolish world around me. You've ruined my fun." Her wee fists pummeled his chest. She'd landed facing him, and her sweet aroma was torturing him. She smelled like flowers and sunshine and the Highlands. What better aroma could there be?

But it was more and he knew it. Lily, the scent that greeted him was his Lily. He'd recognize it anywhere. Just as he was about to answer her, an arrow flew past them, hitting the tree just beyond them. He slowed his horse and turned around in time to see Gwyneth and Logan rushing toward him.

"Where are you taking her, Maule? Unhand my niece." Logan's bellow was fierce enough to stop him in his tracks. His horse danced a little as Lily tried her best to turn around and face forward.

"He ruined my fun. I was just trying to forget all my troubles, and he had to come along and ruin everything. Just like he always does. I hate you, Kyle Maule."

Kyle was stunned by her declaration, and not a little fearful of Logan Ramsay. "What have I done wrong? I was just protecting the chieftain's sister as I've been charged to do."

Gwyneth brought her horse up close to him. "Aye, but you acted rashly. Logan and I were within an arrow's distance from her. We are capable of taking care of her."

"I did not see Logan. Forgive me." Kyle's head spun with all the ramifications he might face for having acted so carelessly. He could not help himself—Lily made him daft sometimes.

Logan said, "Aye, I know you had good intentions, but a trained warrior checks the situation carefully before he acts. Your concern for Lily was not wrong, but you acted with no concern for anyone else in the area. You flew through a crowd full of women and bairns with no caution, lad."

Logan was absolutely correct. Kyle's focus had been on Lily and Lily alone. "Forgive me, my lord. My error."

"I know you mean well, Kyle," Gwyneth added, "but do not ever think to crush her spirit. My niece's spirit is a treasure to me and many others. We delight in it because 'tis a boon to our souls."

Lily jumped down from the horse almost in tears. Sniffling, she ran over to her horse, calling out, "Tilly, come here, Tilly."

As soon as she mounted and headed back toward the keep, Kyle glanced at Logan and Gwyneth. "Tilly? Is that not Sunshine?"

"Not any longer," Gwyneth said. "She felt the need to change her name from Sunshine to Tilly." She pursed her lips and glowered at him. "I'd like you to think on why that could be." With that, Gwyneth turned her horse around and headed back to Molly, Maggie, and Sorcha, who were already mounted and following Lily back to the keep.

Logan quirked a brow at him before he followed Gwyneth. "She changed the name today, lad."

Hellfire, he could do naught right when it came to the lass he loved. He needed to speak with her and apologize. The last time he'd rescued her, she'd clung to him sobbing in fright.

This time, she had run from him in tears.

Lily could hardly see because of the tears blurring her vision. What was wrong with that lad? Why, he had acted like he hated her.

Mayhap it was because her father had tried to talk Kyle into a betrothal he did not want. She didn't know who to be angry with, Kyle or her sire. She rubbed Tilly's mane, hoping to calm her from all the chaos surrounding them. Once at the stable, she moved to dismount, but a warm pair of hands reached up and grasped her around the waist, setting her down on the ground in front of him.

Kyle. She wished to argue with him, but it was no longer in her. Resigned to her fate of being an unlikeable lass, she pushed him aside and headed back toward the keep.

"Och, nay. You'll not dismiss me so easily, Lily. I need to speak with you." He tugged her arm, pulling her back toward him.

"Leave me be, Kyle. You've hurt me enough for one day."

"Lily, forgive me for being so rash. I should not have stopped you, but I was afraid your attacker would return. Wait. How have I hurt you? I never meant to hurt you. Did I twist your arm or something when I lifted you onto my horse?" He looked at each of her hands in turn.

By now, she noticed they had a small audience because Gwyneth, Logan, and her cousins had also returned to the stables, along with a few of the villagers. Logan was trying to send the villagers on their way, but they were hanging back to catch their conversation. She did not care. She would speak her mind, with or without the audience.

"How did you hurt me? As if you did not know. Well, I suppose you do not know that *I* know."

"What?" He dropped his hands from her.

Lily could see the confusion on his face, so she made a bold decision. She would no longer hide the fact that she had eavesdropped and knew all. "I know what transpired."

"Lily, what are you talking about?" His hands settled on his hips.

Lily stared up at the man to whom she'd given her heart to long ago, his dark hair wild from the wind, his blue eyes locked on hers and full of pain. Pain? He truly did look hurt about something. Well, it could not have anything to do with her, so she continued. "I know, Kyle. I *know*." She did all she could to keep the tears at bay, vowing not to let him see how upset she was.

"Know what?"

She could almost see a veil of fear descend over his eyes. Her voice dropped to a whisper. "I overheard someone talking about you. I know my father asked you if you would accept a betrothal to me."

His eyes widened and his mouth fell open, but he said naught. She heard a gasp from behind that indicated her cousins taking in their conversation.

Her voice caught in the middle of her next sentence. "I know you refused me. I suppose I am not good enough for you. I'm heir to naught, so you do not want me. If 'tis the way you want it, then so be it, but please keep your hands away from me. Never touch me again." She fought her tears and finally became angry instead. What had this man done to her?

"You have it all wrong, Lily. 'Tis not why I said nay."

She ignored him. "I think 'tis probably just as well. I've never been as angry and upset as you've made me. 'Tis best for you to be out of my life. I'm going straight to my brother to request that you no longer be assigned to protect me. I know 'tis a job you've hated, so you are now relieved of it."

Kyle stood rooted to his place, unable to speak. Finally, he understood. She glanced over his shoulder to see the sympathetic look in her cousins' eyes and the shock on her aunt's face. Aunt Gwyneth had probably just now realized she'd overheard her private discussion in the stables. It did not matter anymore.

She spun around and headed toward the keep, hoping to locate her brother quickly.

Once inside the great hall, she made her way over to the solar and rapped on the door.

"Enter." Recognizing her sire's voice, she opened the door. Her sire and Torrian were the only two in the room, sitting at their desks. Uncle Logan, Aunt Gwyneth, and Kyle were trailing behind her, but they stopped outside of the solar.

Uncle Logan stuck his head in the door and said, "I believe 'twould help you if you let us all come inside."

Lily did not care, as long as this ended her connection with Kyle.

Lily's brother motioned to her. "Lily, is this acceptable to you?"

She nodded, her arms crossed in front of her, though she had to swipe at her tears every so often. Hell, but why did that lad make her soul ache? She wished to dig a hole into the floor and climb in, never to talk to another person.

Moving deeper into the room, she came to a stop in front of her brother. Her arms were still crossed in front of her, but now she flexed her fingers as she thought of slapping Kyle silly.

"My lairds," Kyle began.

Torrian shook his head and held his arm out to Kyle, indicating that he was not ready to listen to him yet.

"Lily?"

She leaned her head back, trying to control her tears, and began. "I would like to request that Kyle be removed as my protector. You are the laird, I am your sister, so he continuously feels the need to protect me. I want it ended." Her chin lifted a notch when she finished.

Her sire said, "Your brother's second does indeed have the job to protect our family. That includes you, Lily. 'Tis not something that can be ended."

"Is there also something written in our traditions, Papa, about what to do when the chieftain's second refuses a betrothal to the chieftain's sister? Because if there is naught about how to handle such a situation, there needs to be."

Her father asked, "How did you..."

"Does it matter, Papa? I know. I know Kyle refused the offer, so I respectfully request that he no longer be considered one of my guards."

Quade stared at Logan. "What do you know of this?"

Logan replied. "I know not how she found out, but Kyle is a bit rash when it comes to protecting Lily."

"Papa," she interrupted. "It does not matter how I know. I know. Either consider my request or I'll find someone willing to escort me to Uncle Alex's. I'm sure my cousins would welcome me at Clan Grant. I can no longer tolerate Kyle Maule's presence." She'd never experienced such rage before, so she knew not how to deal with it. What could she do? Her entire clan would know that Kyle had refused her. She wished to punch him and scratch him and kick him, all at once. How could someone she loved hurt her so badly?

"I'll go to the Grants." That was the last statement she had to add to the discussion.

All five faces turned to stare at her as if they could read her thoughts. She knew she had threatened the one thing they could not argue. Ever since she was young, she'd been a favorite of Uncle Alex's. He would never turn her down. She quirked her brow at her brother and said, "Well? What is your decision? I'll not be changing my mind."

CHAPTER SEVEN

Torrian crossed the bailey with Kyle the following morn. "Uncle Logan said he'd meet us in the lists."

"Will you tell me what this is about? Is he going to beat me or something? He was not happy with me yesterday. I have no doubt the man is capable of giving me an arse whipping over your sister."

"I think there are a few people ready to give you an arse whipping," Torrian grumbled. "I've never seen my sire more upset than when she said she wished to move to Clan Grant. I had no choice but to assign someone else to protect her. Believe me when I say you must do as you've been ordered."

"But how did she find out about your father's request?"

Torrian shrugged. "It does not matter. She found out, as oft happens when such a thing is discussed."

"I'd like to talk to her and explain my reasoning."

"I'm sure you would, but you've been warned to stay away from her. And I'll warn you that if you chase Lily away to Clan Grant, my sire and uncle will be less than happy. Consider this your last chance to make things right. You did not want her, so stay away."

"But you know 'tis not why I turned your sire down."

"Kyle." Torrian stopped to turn to his friend. "I admit my part in this travesty. My sire did ask me if you were interested in anyone special, or if I thought you were interested in Lily. I should have guessed his intent, but I had my mind on other things. But I must admit, you took me by surprise with your refusal. I would never force you to act against your conscience. You've made your decision. Now you must accept that you cannot have it both ways.

You cannot continue to spend time with my sister without hurting her."

"But 'tis not how I feel." The truth was, this wasn't just about honoring his father. How could he possibly explain to his friend how much he feared the thought of marrying his love? He did not take his responsibilities to the clan lightly. He always did his best, but would that even be possible if he were married to Lily? How could he think clearly if he lived with Lily and had to worry about someone hurting or kidnapping her? "Torrian, you know I must first make my sire proud. You know what he asked of me when he was dying, to become the best Ramsay warrior I could be."

"I understand your point of view, but you must understand Lily's. You rejected her. 'Tis the only way she will see it. I'm sure you can comprehend that. I would leave everything alone for a while. Allow matters to settle, or so my sire often advises. Lily will get over you."

"I'll stay away unless I see her in trouble. You know I'll not be able to stay away under those circumstances." Hellfire, what had he done? He did not want his life to exist without Lily in it.

And he did *not* want Lily to get over him.

"*If* you see her in trouble. Those are the key words. Dancing in a meadow with a crowd of Ramsays around does not count."

"Aye, I understand I erred that day. She makes me daft sometimes." He hung his head, not knowing what he should do next. Could they not see how hard he was trying to be the best second possible? Was his father watching this fiasco from heaven?

Logan appeared out of nowhere. "If a lass makes you daft, you should not turn down the offer of a betrothal. You should make her yours."

Kyle didn't respond, mostly because he did not know how. They had not been there that day when his father had begged him to make him proud by becoming a Ramsay warrior. As the chief's second, he'd exceeded even his own expectations, and he had no desire to stop.

Logan said, "Since you're the chieftain's second, I would like to spar with you and see if you need any more training."

"Is this because of the other day, my lord?" Kyle couldn't bring himself to look Logan in the eye because he believed he'd failed him so.

"What other day? You mean chasing after my niece as if you were addled? Nay, 'tis because you protect my clan, and you need to be strong. No more." Logan found a spot and pulled his tunic off, leaving himself in just his plaid to fight. He unsheathed his sword and stared at Kyle with a gleam in his eye. "Are you ready, lad? Show me what skills you have."

Kyle took a deep breath as he unsheathed his sword and removed his tunic. He wiped the sweat from his brow and took his stance opposite Logan Ramsay, waiting for him to start.

Logan parried with him for half an hour before he stopped, holding his hand up to Kyle in a motion for him to do the same. "Not bad, lad, but you do not have the drive in you yet. Tell me how you would attack someone you caught kissing my niece."

Kyle halted, wiping his face with his plaid. "I'm not allowed around your niece, if you recall. So that will never happen."

Logan chuckled, as did Torrian. "Word around the clan is that Lily is open to aught who wants her. I heard a group of three lads discussing her near the stable last eve, and I tell you they are ready to go after her now that you're no longer interested in her."

"What?" Kyle's body tensed at the thought of another lad with Lily. He ground his teeth to keep from saying what he wished to say.

"Everyone suspected your heart was lost to her for the last couple of years. I believe even Lily knew in her own way. 'Twas the way you looked at her. No one would approach her."

Caught off-guard by this revelation, Kyle glanced at Torrian in bafflement. They'd all known?

Torrian nodded. "Aye, I suspected. Nay, I was sure, which is why you took me by surprise when you turned my sire down."

Kyle stared at both of them. "And who are the lads you heard discussing her?"

"I'll not tell you," Logan said, "but I believe Lily will definitely be interested in one of them."

"You agree, Torrian?" Kyle peered at his friend.

"Aye, she'll go for one of them. She's hurting at present. You broke her heart."

The image of Lily kissing another lad crossed his vision, and a fury set in him he'd never felt before.

Logan said to Torrian, "Did the lad not say he wanted to do

more than kiss Lily? What did he say again?"

Kyle swung his sword with both of his arms, hefting it into the sky with a deep guttural cry, and went at Logan with all his might.

Logan laughed. "Now you're ready, lad."

When it dawned on Kyle that Logan had planned this ruse to build his ire, he became even angrier. They parried, steel hitting steel, sending an occasional spark shooting into the air. Kyle went at Logan with all his might, gritting his teeth as he thought about another lad kissing his Lily. His dark hair was now plastered to his head from his sweat, and he decided to end the game. Logan Ramsay had been a great swordsman in his day, but he didn't have the strength he used to possess.

Kyle's aggression increased because he was sure he'd beat the man. If he did, Lily and Torrian would both see what a great warrior he'd become. How he wished his sire could see him, too. He swung his sword in a wide arc to knock the weapon out of Logan's hands.

Except Logan did a quick, last-minute maneuver Kyle hadn't expected. A loud thwack hit Kyle's hands on the hilt of his sword, and his weapon went flying through the air before landing with a thud at Torrian's feet. With another blow, Logan knocked him flat on his arse.

"Lad, you must listen to me," the older man said, standing over him with his sword pointed at his belly. "When you love a lass, she'll only dig at your soul until you admit it and make her yours."

Kyle gasped for air, stunned to have lost to a man he'd been sure he could beat. "Nay, thinking on her, marrying her will make me weak. Can you not see that? You've just proven it." He waited for Logan to stand back and admit he was right. If he had not been thinking about Lily and his sire, he would have won for sure.

Logan chuckled, shaking his head. "Nay, lad. 'Tis where you're wrong. The right lass will only make you stronger. My wife has made me stronger and wiser than I ever could have been on my own." He sheathed his sword and offered Kyle a hand to help him up. "Let me know when you are ready to seriously consider my words."

Kyle stared at Logan's back as he walked away, stymied by his declaration. Still panting, he glanced at his friend.

Torrian nodded at him. "Every word is true."

Lily sat at the dais, staring down at the crowd. Her sire had relented and ordered Kyle to stay away from her, and he had done as ordered.

Now her heart ached more and more each day. She shouldn't have sent him away. As far back as she could remember, Kyle had always been nearby. He and Torrian were best friends, so she'd always known where to find him. Now she'd lost her protector, her friend, and her source of comfort. Why?

She had to remind herself that Kyle was the one who had rejected her. Sorcha, Maggie, and Molly came over to her side of the dais once the minstrels and fiddlers had arrived. Her sire had called for a night of entertainment. She knew not why, but she hoped it would take her mind off her troubles.

Maggie said, "We tried to get Bethia to come down, but she refused. Why does she not spend more time with us?"

"Bethia is shy and verra devoted to healing. You know she's not at ease in crowds." Lily propped her elbow on the table and cradled her chin in her hand, staring out at the gathering.

"Tell us about what you saw when you found Davina and Ranulf again. I love hearing that story," Sorcha said with a sigh. Then she glanced over her shoulder, probably to ensure their elders were not nearby.

"Why?" Lily asked.

"Because I like hearing it."

Molly laughed. "Sorcha, you're too young."

"Nay, I know all about what a lass and a lad do. But I like to hear the way Lily tells it." She waited expectantly.

When Molly and Maggie grinned at her too, urging her to tell the tale yet again, Lily decided to appease her cousins. "He was disgusting."

"But did you see it? All of it?" Sorcha's elbows rested on the table as she leaned forward eagerly.

"Of course. I told you I interrupted them in the middle. And then Ranulf came toward me and asked me to join them."

"What did he say again?" asked Maggie.

"He said he'd be sure to please me."

Molly leaned forward and whispered in her ear, "I just wish to know if you were tempted."

"Nay!" Lily was appalled by Molly's suggestion. True, her cousin was quite a bit older than her, but nevertheless...

Sorcha and Maggie giggled.

"Why not? Molly asked in a louder voice, her eyes dancing.

"Because he was disgusting. And so was she. I would never have allowed him to touch me."

"I do not blame you. He was disturbing, almost sinister." Maggie narrowed her gaze. "What about her? Did she want him to touch you?"

"Nay. She was jealous."

Then Sorcha brought up the one thing Lily usually avoided talking about. "What did it look like? How big was it?"

"You've all seen the horses. I do not know why you tease me so. It was big and it jutted right out. I've told you all I'm going to tell you."

All three lasses broke into gales of laughter. Lily had been annoyed by Sorcha's request to tell the story of how she'd caught the two lovers, especially since she'd shared it with her cousins time and again, but she was enjoying the merriment. "And..."

All three stopped their clatter in an instant and leaned toward her. "And *what*?"

Lily knew just how to bait them. "And the more he walked, the more it shrunk."

Sorcha squealed and jumped in her seat.

"And once it shrunk, it started wiggling and bouncing all over the place."

All three of them hopped out of their seats and guffawed, making a racket that was drawing attention from across the great hall. Lily just sat back and watched her cousins in amusement. She did love them, and it felt good to make them laugh. Of course, it hadn't been funny the day she'd walked in on Ranulf and Davina. She'd just stared at his male parts in shock, which is why she thought he'd invited her to join them. Of course, she wasn't about to admit that to her cousins.

Nor would she admit how many times she'd thought of doing that same act with Kyle. In truth, she was jealous of how close Ranulf and Davina had been, how they'd looked like one person in the bed. What would it be like? The intensity of the act had shocked her, but she wished to share the same thing with the love of her life. Her cousins brought her out of her trance.

"What happened when Kyle came in again?" Maggie asked.

"He grabbed me by the shoulders and shoved me toward the door." Lily played with the linen square on the table.

"Lily, you must stop pining for Kyle," Sorcha said. "He'll be back."

Lily took a deep breath and said to her cousin, "I'm not pining for Kyle. I'm quite happy today. Actually, I was thinking I need to kiss another lad. Who shall I choose?" Her gaze searched the hall for just the right lad, skipping past the largest lad in the hall, for the sight of his dark hair threatened to make her sigh aloud. She caught a glance of Kyle out of the corner of her eye, looking a bit haunted and unhappy, but she ignored him and moved on to the other unmarried lads in the hall.

"Lily? Truly?" Sorcha's eyes widened and she bounced in her seat. "Who would you like to kiss? They'd all love to kiss you."

Maggie added, "You could choose any one you want, and..."

"And what?" Lily asked.

Molly leaned toward her, her voice dropping to a whisper. "If you kiss another, Kyle will get verra jealous."

Sorcha's hand flew to her mouth to hide her gasp, but then she nodded. "I think you should do it. He will get upset."

Lily thought for a moment as she perused the hall full of lads. A quick glance over her shoulder told her that Torrian was so entranced by Heather he was paying her no attention at all, and her sire had gone above stairs, probably because his knee pained him so. Mayhap her cousins were right. She could not deny she wished to make Kyle jealous. Would he not recognize the error in his ways if he saw her kissing another? Would he not wish to push the lad away from her and wrap his arms around her instead?

She tapped her fingers on the table, considering the possibility, and then leaned in toward her cousins. "Nay, 'twill not work. Kyle only yells at me of late. He will not care. He yelled at me yesterday morn because I distracted his guards. He yelled at me when he found me out in the meadow after I was chased by the man in chain mail. He yells at me so much that he will not give a care at all."

Sorcha leaned toward her, poking a finger at her. "You deserved to be yelled at for running in the meadow alone. My sire would tie me to the stables if I ever did such a thing."

Molly agreed. "Aye, you should not run alone. But trust me, you'll make him jealous."

Lily pinched her lips together as she glanced about the hall. "I think not. He will not care, and that will hurt me more."

"He will care," Molly said, "but we can leave him out of it. Do you not wish to see how another lad kisses?"

She jerked her head back to Molly. "Why? How many have you kissed?"

Her cousin snorted. "Enough to know I want no one here."

Lily's mouth fell open. "You've kissed more than one or two?"

Once Molly nodded with a chuckle, Lily peered at Maggie. "And you, too?"

"Lily, Maggie and I are a wee bit older than you. Of course I have. Sorcha's a few years younger than you, and she's already kissed a few. You've missed out because you've saved yourself for Kyle. 'Tis time to change that. And if it makes him jealous? All the better."

Sorcha patted her hand. "And you're the chieftain's daughter."

"*Sister*. I'm the chieftain's sister, a role that no longer carries any importance, I must remind you."

"Only in your mind, Lily. Do not belittle yourself just because your brother married." Molly fussed with her hair, brushing her wild curls back from her face. "Once the lads discover Kyle is no longer interested in you, they'll be around you like honey bees."

"Molly, you have such an imagination. The lads already know Kyle's not interested, and do you see any bees around me?"

"You have no idea of your worth, do you? Have you not looked at your reflection? The only reason they have not flocked around you is because Kyle still stands in the hall. If there's even a chance the laird's second fancies you, they know he'll make them pay in the lists on the morrow."

She still did not think Kyle would be jealous, but mayhap it was time for her to grow up, to explore life a bit more. Any one of the lads would suit, but she had to choose carefully. Her gaze narrowed on three in particular. "Aye, I see the wisdom of your words, but how could I possibly choose one? And how would I ask him for a kiss? The lad must do the chasing, not the lass."

Maggie waggled her eyebrows at Lily. "We'll take care of it for you. You name the place and we'll send a lad or two your way. Trust me, they'll all want to follow you."

Lily twisted her hands in her lap. "I'm not usually that forward. And I have no idea who to choose."

"What about Bothan or Cawley?"

"Aye, I like Cawley. Or what about Henson?" Sorcha asked.

"I suppose Cawley is braw." Her gaze crossed the hall again, dissatisfied with her choice, but she knew exactly what the problem was. None of them had dark brown hair and deep blue eyes, eyes that reached deep into her soul, eyes that could curl her toes, eyes that only searched for hers.

"Cawley it is," Molly said. "We'll not give you time to back down. Where, Lily? Where shall we tell him to meet you?"

Lily frowned, trying to think of exactly the right place, but came up with naught. She did not wish to get caught.

"Outside in the bailey, but where?" Lily chewed on her finger in thought.

"By the bench in the far corner. No one is ever there," Sorcha whispered.

"Nay, I wish to be able to hide if I change my mind. And I do not wish to be caught by my aunt or uncle. You know how your sire is."

"Where? Just name your place?" Molly said. "Da is jesting with Gavin and Gregor. He'll not bother you. I think he's had a few ales."

"All right. Outside Tilly's stall."

Sorcha grinned, but Molly's smile left her face completely. Molly said, "You cannot do it there. 'Tis not safe. What if he tried to take advantage? What if he wanted more than a kiss? We will get in trouble if aught happens besides a kiss."

"That's where it will be. I'm not worried about Cawley, he's not that bold, and Tilly is still in the stall with two entrances. Tell him to meet me at the outside door to Tilly's stall in about half an hour."

Sorcha whispered, "We'll go with you."

"Nay," Lily ground out. "I do not need you three watching. I'll do this alone."

"Nay," Maggie said calmly as she looked around the hall. "We'll not be far. If you are in trouble, just scream. Now, we're going to talk to Cawley. You go."

They bolted out of their seats before Lily could stop them.

There was no changing her mind now.

CHAPTER EIGHT

Lily kissed Tilly's neck. "Nay, Tilly, not this eve, but someday soon I'll braid your mane again with pretty ribbons." She always knew what her horse was thinking. "Now you must be quiet, my sweet. Do not scare him away." She combed her horse's fur, humming a quiet tune, one she hoped would calm her own beating heart.

She'd chosen Tilly's stall because it had two doors, one to the outside and one to the stable corridor. Was she out of her mind? Nay, she needed to know. Kyle had tasted delicious, and she'd felt so safe and cherished whenever his arms had wrapped around her. Yet he had rejected her. Why had her sire ruined everything by forcing the issue?

A whisper interrupted her thoughts. "Lily?"

Lily jumped at Cawley's voice, but squared her shoulders, brushed her hands on her gown, and made her way over to the door. She unlatched it and opened it for Cawley. "Aye?"

"Molly said you would let me kiss you. 'Tis true?" His face held the happiest expression she'd ever seen.

Lily surveyed Cawley's messy red hair, his freckles, and the smile on his face. He was truly good-hearted, so he would be safe enough. She nodded, and before she could even tip her lips up to him, he wrapped his arms around her and tugged her close, covering her lips with his. He ground his mouth against hers, pushing at her lips with his tongue as saliva collected on her cheek and her chin. She shoved at his chest, not wanting his wet tongue inside of her mouth since it reminded her of the lapping tongue of one of her brother's Deerhounds. He stepped back, a wide grin on his face, and she said, "Enough, Cawley."

He jumped as he stepped back, his gaze locked on hers. "I cannot believe it. I love you truly, Lily."

As he raced down the side of the stables with a low whistle, Lily wiped his saliva from her cheek and retreated to the safety of her horse's stall. She glanced at her horse, a scowl on her face, "Tilly, I believe you would kiss better than that. Our plan is failing. This makes me want Kyle's kisses even more."

Before she could turn around, another voice greeted her from the doorway. "Lily, 'tis true? You'll allow a kiss?" Henson stood in front of her, hopping from one foot to the other as he awaited her answer.

She shrugged her shoulders and made her way to the door, though she halted and stared at Henson first. "Do not slobber on me, Henson."

He paled. "Nay, never, my lady."

She cautiously leaned toward him, allowing herself room to back away if necessary. "And no hands, Henson."

He nodded vehemently, thrusting his hands behind his back. "Whatever you say."

She leaned forward and his lips settled on hers, warm and wet.

And he tasted like boar meat. She yanked back, forcing herself not to spit in front of him. Henson was a nice lad—he just happened to taste like a boar or a hedgehog. She was not quite sure since she'd never tasted a hedgehog before. But surely it would bring to mind the flavor of Henson's kisses.

"Many thanks, Lily. 'Twas a good kiss, was it not?"

The hope in his gaze forced her to do something she instantly regretted. Saying a quick prayer begging for forgiveness for the lie she was about to tell, she stared at him and said, "Aye, Henson. 'Twas nice." She ticked another count on her fingers behind her back. Was that lie number five or six? Tilly snorted and dragged her front foot across the dirt a couple of times. Lily swung her head around and glared at her dear horse. "Tilly, must you remind me of my failings? All right, I'll add another." Tilly's hoof stomped again. "Aye, *two* more, if I must." She dragged her gaze back to Henson to find him still staring at her, a daft grin plastered to his face.

He smiled and ran off, but not before he said, "Your turn," to the next person by the door.

Your turn? What in hell was he talking about? She stuck her head out the door only to see a line that extended to the end of the stables and beyond. Lads, lads, and more lads. Lads kneading their hands, primping their hair, puffing their chests out, some of them even winking at her.

Fiddle, what had she gotten herself into this time?

Kyle had scowled and frightened away every person who had attempted to talk to him. He'd already spied his Lily sitting at the dais looking lost, but she was alone. How he wished to sit by her side and bring her beautiful smile back to life. Every so often, she would force a smile, but it never reached her eyes, so Kyle knew she was distraught.

How had everything taken such an unwelcome turn? A fortnight ago, he'd been ecstatic with his new life. He'd been appointed as his best friend's second—a promotion that had guaranteed him the right to be around the lass he loved at all times because it was now *his* job to protect her.

It had been wonderful for a short time. Then disaster had struck in the form of Quade Ramsay's betrothal request.

Torrian came up to his side. "Your face tells all."

"What are you talking about?"

"If you frown any more, you'll have deep wrinkles everywhere on your face. We all know why you're unhappy."

Kyle glared at his friend. "If you know so much, then why did you not warn me about what your sire would ask of me?"

"Because I did not know. He asked me about your interests, but he never mentioned a betrothal. Lily is his daughter, not mine."

"But now she hates me." He cast a quick glance her way, unable to stop himself.

"Then why did you turn my sire down? I always secretly believed you loved my sister, and I know she has feelings for you. I think you'd be perfect together." Torrian shrugged his shoulders.

Kyle turned to face him directly. "I do not wish to give up my job as your second."

"But no one ever said you needed to. You can marry and still be my second."

"Torrian, I see how you are with your new wife. Your mind is often wandering. I could not afford that at this early stage. You are the chief's heir. Your position is not at risk from anyone below you, but there are probably many lads waiting to step into my job.

"So you're thinking I would not reward someone who has always been loyal and steadfast?"

"Nay, 'tis not what I'm saying. But would I still be steadfast if I had a lass to take care of all the time, a lass to distract me from my purpose?"

"Aye. I do not see why not. Look around the hall. Plenty of my sire's men are married."

"Seamus never married. Mayhap being second to the laird is too much to handle along with a marriage." Kyle did look around the room, and it seemed there were happy couples everywhere. "Had I been given time to think, I may have asked your sire if I could postpone the betrothal for a year or two until I was ready. It happened too quickly." He rubbed the back of his neck, trying to decide what he should do.

Nay, he had no idea if he was capable of staying away from her without making himself miserable. Already, his chest hurt so much that he wished to heave.

"I got married and took on the job of chieftain at the same time." Torrian clasped his friend on the shoulder. "Think on it, Kyle. My sire has not betrothed her to anyone else. I know that Lily misses you. Reconsider your answer to my sire. I'm sure he would consider delaying the wedding, but not by two years." He clasped his shoulder. "While you're doing that, why not enjoy the company of another lass? I see plenty here who have been watching you." Torrian tipped his head in the direction of two lasses staring at Kyle.

"Nay, I'm not interested in either of them," Kyle shouted, almost loud enough for the entire hall to hear him.

"Proves my point." Torrian winked at him before he sauntered away. "I knew you'd say nay. You cannot live your life refusing all."

Kyle uncrossed his arms and tried to adjust his expression. Sorcha, Maggie, and Molly had sat down next to Lily, and they had her smiling again. He forced himself to look away—something that was getting harder and harder. Was his friend correct? Were others lasses interested in him? He glanced around the room, only to discover Torrian was correct. There were quite a few lasses looking in his direction. He had never paid them much attention before.

He moved over to the table at the end of the hall to grab another goblet of ale. Many were dancing tonight, but he was not in the mood. All of a sudden, three lasses stepped in front of him.

"Good eve to you, Kyle." A dark-haired lass fluttered her lashes at him.

"Good eve."

"You do not look happy. What is troubling you?"

He took a sip of his ale. "Naught. I'm having a good time. Are you not?"

"Well, we were hoping you would dance with us. You could take turns since there are three of us."

Kyle gave them a lop-sided grin. "You want me to dance with all three of you?"

"Not at the same time," the second lass giggled.

But even their bawdy teasing could not distract him. He found himself glancing around the hall, which was when he discovered that Lily had disappeared.

The dark-haired lass whispered, "Are you seeking out Lily?"

He shook his head, quickly denying the truth. How the hell had they known that?

"Have you not heard what Lily is doing this eve?"

The lasses giggled in unison, a sight Kyle had rarely seen. Three hands rose to cover three giggles at the same moment. He was so distracted by watching the three of them together, it took a moment for their question to register. "Lily? What do you mean? She was just at the dais a few moments ago."

The dark-haired lass, clearly the leader of the group, responded with a delighted expression and a smug tone he did not like. "Lily's giving kisses to anyone who wants one."

Kyle thought the top of his head would shoot off and hit the highest beam for sure. He struggled to control his emotions and managed to say, "What? Would you repeat that?"

"Lily. I heard she's giving kisses to any lad who wishes for one."

Struggling to keep his fury in check, he ground out between clenched teeth. "Where is she?"

"At the stables. We did not think you would be interested since you two are not talking. Everyone in the clan knows that," the red-haired lass finally said. "But many lads are interested in kissing Lily."

Kyle thrust his empty goblet at one of the pretty lasses and turned to rush toward the door without a backward glance. He started counting, something his mother had taught him to do whenever his anger or impatience got the best of him. Usually it worked, but he'd be counting to a thousand before it ever worked this eve. Visions of a crowd of lads with their hands on Lily clustered in the darkest corner of his brain, and he could not free himself from it.

CHAPTER NINE

Lily wiped the back of her hand across her mouth just as the world outside the stables erupted in chaos. She'd gone back inside to hide from all the lads, hoping Tilly would give her an idea on how to evade the line of lads waiting for her. "Just you wait until I see Maggie, Sorcha, and Molly again. Look what they've done to me."

That sentence had barely left her mouth when a ruckus started up outside. She crept over to the door to peek out, just in time to see Kyle pick Henson up with a roar and toss him over in front of a nearby tree. He went after three more lads, punching and tossing his way through them before the rest of the lads realized that an enraged Kyle Maule was headed their way.

Some stayed to watch, but most took off. Lily headed out the door and started yelling at him. "Kyle, stop. You'll hurt them and 'tis not their fault."

"Not their fault? Taking advantage of a foolish lass *is* their fault." He hauled his fist back and punched a lad leaping at him. Two more were behind him.

Lily ducked and stepped back. "I'm not foolish. I knew what I wanted."

A lad yelled, "Maule, go home. She's no longer yours and she agreed to kiss us all."

Lily's hands went directly to her hips. "Fiddle on you. I did no such thing, Bryce. Do not be telling fibs about me. You have not spoken to me once."

Cawley yelled from a spot in the back. "But you said you'd kiss any lad who wanted a kiss."

Lily's face dropped to stare at the ground. "Fiddle on you all and leave me be, please."

Kyle jumped on Cawley. "I'll knock your teeth out for saying such a thing about her."

"She's not yours, Maule. Leave us alone to have some fun," another yelled.

Kyle punched the two lads who came at him next, then jumped another pair of warriors, pummeling them while he held them down on the ground. "The hell she isn't. She's been mine for a long time. You'll all keep your hands off her or you'll deal with me." Two others attacked him, so he stood and hit both of them, one in the jaw and one in the belly. Hoisting a third into the air, he tossed him toward two others off to the side, felling them all. "Who else? Come on, foolish whoresons. I'll beat the shite out of anyone who dares to touch her or who says aught bad about her."

Molly, Maggie, and Sorcha ran up to Lily. "What happened?"

"Kyle found out," Lily said. "And some friends you are. Why did you tell them I'd kiss anyone?"

Molly shook her head. "We did not say that. We only told Cawley and Henson."

Sorcha nodded. "'Struth."

The bulk of the lads had moved off and Kyle stood there panting, his hands dripping blood that he wiped on his plaid. After he was sure the lads were gone, he turned to her. "Lily, are you hurt?"

Lily moved over to him. "Nay, Kyle, but why did you do that?"

Her cousins exchanged a look and took off toward the keep without another word.

Lily picked up Kyle's bloodied hand and kissed his knuckle. "You should not have done that. I did say I would kiss one of them."

He quirked his brow at her. "And did you enjoy it?"

Lily frowned. "I'll not discuss it, but you turned me down. I need to think of others. I do not wish to spend my life alone."

Kyle turned and wrapped his arms around her. "Och, Lily, you'll not be alone. I've tried to talk to you, but you're always mad. 'Tis not you, but if I had you to come home to each night, I'd never work."

She rested her head on his shoulder and said, "You broke my heart, Kyle Maule, and I do not know if it'll ever be fixed."

Kyle's hands threaded through her hair. "You know my sire asked me to be a Ramsay warrior. And then I'd be leaving you, and how could I do that? Who would protect my wife if I had to go out and fight? If you were my wife, you'd distract me terribly and I'd be an awful second."

A brusque voice shouted out. "Looks to me like she's distracting you plenty when you're not married. How could it be any worse?"

Lily lifted her head to see Uncle Logan leaning against a nearby tree. "Uncle, must you interrupt us?"

"Aye, someone needed to come out here. There are stories floating into the keep about one of our guards tearing limbs from half our guards in training. We need those lads."

Kyle dropped his hands from Lily and said, "My apologies, my lord. Seems I've lost control again."

"I'd say you have, Maule. Did you put an end to whatever was driving your fury?"

"Aye." Kyle hung his head.

Logan walked over to Lily and held his arm out to her. "I'll escort you back to the keep, lass."

Lily turned to Kyle and said, "My thanks for always being my protector."

Kyle gave her a sheepish look, rubbing his raw knuckles.

Logan grasped his shoulder and said, "I can promise you, 'twill not get any better for you, lad, until you accept what you feel."

Once again, Lily found herself sitting in front of her family in the solar. Her sire, her stepmother, Logan, Gwyneth, and Torrian were all gathered in the room, sitting and staring at her.

Her sire started, "I'd like an explanation for the events of last night, daughter. Your mama had many wounds to deal with this morn."

Lily hung her head. "Forgive me, but I used poor judgement last night. I agreed to kiss another lad. The offer was misconstrued, several lads showed up at the stables, and Kyle found out about it."

"How many did you agree to kiss, Lily?" Torrian asked.

Lily sat up straight, her hands grabbing the arms of the chair in which she sat. "I only agreed to kiss one. 'Twas not my fault it was misinterpreted."

"Our daughters had a hand in this, my laird," Gwyneth added. "'Twas not all Lily's fault."

"You know randy lads," Logan said. "Once they hear something, it tends to get a bit twisted, and Kyle did not like it at all."

"Aught else you'd like to add, daughter?" Quade asked as he folded his hands on his lap.

Lily didn't like that move. That meant he was about to reveal some decision he'd made. What was his plan for her now? Did one kiss…or two…mean they would expect her to change her life again? Go on more healing expeditions with her mama or shoot more arrows? This was becoming too exhausting. She just wished to be left alone, to enjoy her pet and the creatures of the forest. She answered her sire, "Nay, naught else."

"Good, then I've come to a decision. I've considered this for a while now, and discussed it with your mama. Due to present circumstances, I believe it is a sound decision."

Lily leaned forward, afraid to learn what judgment was to be passed on her now.

"Uncle Logan and Aunt Gwyneth have decided to take Molly and Sorcha to Edinburgh. Each of the lasses have expressed an interest in working for the crown, so they will travel to court to observe it a bit more closely. I'm sending you with them."

Lily could not believe her ears. "You're sending me away?"

"Aye, I believe you need to get away from Ramsay land for a wee bit. We still do not know who attempted to kidnap you. This worries me, daughter. I'll not have you at risk. If we send you away, we'll be certain naught will happen to you. You'll have much protection and you'll wander less in an unknown location. I know you too well."

"But I do not wish to go, Papa. I did not like it when we were there before."

Aunt Gwyneth said, "Sorcha and Molly love to travel, and they'll enjoy having you along. Do you not think it would be nice to get away for a wee bit?"

Lily shook her head. "Nay. I hated seeing the Buchans and all those daft people in the royal burgh. I like my home. Must I go? And what if that man who chased me in the meadow knows and follows me?"

"You'll be leaving on the morrow, Lily," Quade said. "You have nothing to fear from the stranger in the meadow. I'll be sending you with your own guard, and he'll be by your side at all times."

"What?" Lily's eyes misted. "There will be a lad with me wherever I go?"

"Aye, and do not look so defeated. You'll be much safer that way. I'll not risk your well-being, daughter, but my decision is made."

"Who?" Tears rolled down her cheeks as she awaited her father's response. She swiped at her tears, but they just kept coming. It was as if a supply of tears had built up inside her because she'd gone years without ever shedding one, and now they were always finding their way out, no matter how she tried to stop them. The inside of her head must be like a huge barrel overflowing with water, truly unstoppable. She tipped her head sideways, deciding she might as well give in and let them all pour out.

"Kyle is going to guard you."

"What?" She stood up from her chair, uncertain she'd heard her father correctly. "Kyle? You're sending Kyle with me?"

"Why do you look so unhappy? I thought my choice of guard would please you."

"No one will protect your daughter better than Kyle," Uncle Logan said, nodding. "You've made the right choice, Quade. The lad fought off ten lads by himself. No one will get past him."

"Do you hear your uncle, Lily? 'Tis why I chose him. He'll protect you."

"Oh, Papa. How could you do this to me?" Lily sat back down and put her head in her lap, sobbing. "He'll hate me forever."

Quade pointed to the door. "I'd like to talk to my daughter alone."

The rest of her family shuffled out, but she scarcely even noticed. Kyle would hate her. Once everyone was gone, she lifted her head. "Can you not see, Papa? He'll hate me. He values his job as second more than anything, and you're pulling him away from Torrian to protect me."

"Lily, his job as Torrian's second is to do as he is ordered. Your brother suggested him, and I believe he made the right choice.

Now, come over here please."

She hurried over to her sire. "What is it, Papa? Why are you so upset with me?"

"I'm not upset with you." He tugged her forward. "Come, sit on my lap like you used to."

"Papa, I'm too big for this. I'm not your wee lassie anymore."

"You will always be my wee lassie. Now come over here." She peered at her father, recognizing the look he had when he was not about to budge from his decision.

"But I'll hurt your knee," she said with a sniffle.

"Nay, you will not. I've never seen my Lilykins with so many tears. Please sit with me."

Lily stared at her father. She adored him, so she sat gingerly on his lap. "You must promise to tell me when I'm hurting your knee."

"You'll not hurt me. Now put your head on my shoulder like you used to do and tell me what's troubling you so."

She rested her head on his shoulder, taking in the familiar scent of her father that she knew so well. Suddenly memories of her childhood swept over her, of being so sick her sire had to carry her around. All those times before her stepmother had come along and healed her ran through her mind, of the love of her sire and her grandmother when she'd been so ill. She'd always rested her head on his shoulder, just like she was doing now, because she'd been too weak to hold it upright. Why, this had to be the most comforting spot in the world next to Tilly's neck.

"Do you know what your stepmother said to me after she first met you?"

"Nay." Her fingers settled on the edge of his plaid, brushing across the soft fabric just as she'd done when she was younger.

"She told me she'd never seen such a happy bairn, especially given how ill you were at the time. She said she'd never seen a child toss everything up, then turn to smile at her."

"I did?" Lily whispered.

"Aye, you did. No matter how sick you were, you still smiled. Stole everyone's heart in the keep, that you did, including Alex Grant's. I just wish your mother could have seen all those smiles, but I believe she watches you from heaven. I see her spirit in you often."

"Do you think so?"

"Aye. Your mother adored you, just like your mama does."

She couldn't stop her tears no matter how she tried. Would the barrel inside her never empty?

"Now, would you like to tell me what has made my smiling daughter so sad?" He kissed her forehead and waited for her answer.

She knew it would upset him, but she needed to know. "Papa, why did you ask Kyle about accepting a betrothal without asking me first?"

"Och, lass, even I make mistakes sometimes. Forgive me. I was surprised he turned me down, but once I thought about it, I realized I had mucked it up."

"He broke my heart. 'Struth is I love Kyle. I always have."

"Have you ever shared that with him, Lily?"

"Nay."

"Why not?"

"He's not asked me."

"Well, mayhap you should tell him."

"But I do not wish to look the fool."

"Lily, the lad loves you."

"Nay, he does not. He does not wish to marry me."

She could feel her father heave a sigh from deep in his chest. How she loved him. He had such a quiet strength, and he was almost always right.

"Do you not recall how things were with the two of you when you were still a wee one? Wherever Torrian and Kyle went, you were right behind them. As a matter of fact, I used to be nervous watching you follow them everywhere, afraid Growley would step on you by accident. But after observing the four of you together, I soon realized I had naught to worry about."

"Because Torrian always protected me. I remember. And so would Growley."

"Nay, Lily. If you fell behind, tripped, or did aught at all to risk yourself, there was always a hand there to protect you, but 'twas not Torrian's—'twas Kyle's. He has always watched out for you. I think he's loved you for a verra long time. A lad would not care for a lass the way he has cared for you without having deep feelings for her."

"Then why did he reject me?"

"Did you know Kyle stayed out half the night searching for your Sunshine after the guards failed to locate her?"

"He did?" She swiped the tears away so more could fill her cheeks.

"And they say it took him almost two hours to coax your favorite horse back."

"Kyle did not tell me that. Sunshine can be a wee bit cantankerous sometimes."

"Was he not there to protect you last night?"

"Aye, but he said he could not marry me because I was too distracting for him. And now you're making him go with me. I'll distract him more, and he'll be even angrier…"

"Lass, I rushed him. He needs to come to terms with his feelings in his own ways. The lad has just been given an important assignment as Torrian's second, and though he lost his sire at a young age, he still grieves that loss every day. He does not have a large family, only his mama."

"But he would if he married me. He'd have all of you."

"Aye, 'tis true, and I believe once he thinks on it, he'll know it, too. We must give him time."

"Papa, must I go to Edinburgh?"

"Aye, I would like you to go with your aunt and uncle."

"But I do not like being away from you and Torrian and Mama. You're my everything."

"I know that, lass, but you must grow up, so I'm sending you away with people I trust. I think 'twill be good for you. And I need to know that my wee Lily is safe. We still know naught of the man in the forest."

"Poor Kyle. I feel bad for him that he does not have his papa to talk to like I do."

"I do, too. His sire was a fine man, and a strong Ramsay warrior. Now that the issue of your trip has been settled, we can head out to the stables and practice your favorite activity, but I'd like to wait until your tears have stopped."

Lily took a few moments, then sat up, wiped her cheeks, and smiled at her father. "I'm ready now, Papa."

He kissed her forehead and said, "Good, now come with me. We're off to the stables, and you must promise me not to tell anyone about this."

"I promise."

He took her hand and led her out the door, just like he had done when she was young.

CHAPTER TEN

Lily grabbed her satchel, threw her mantle over her arm, and marched out her chamber door and down the stairs to the hall to break her fast before they started their journey. At the base of the stairs, she took a deep breath and made her way to the table.

She heard three gasps, saw two people raise their hands to their mouths, and almost everyone stared wide-eyed at her.

"Good morn to you, daughter." Quade's gaze narrowed, but he said naught about her change. "You are ready for your journey to begin?"

"Aye. My thanks for sending me, Papa. I'm sure 'twill be wonderful." She chastised herself right away. Another lie. Fiddle, but at least Tilly was not here to witness it.

"My thanks for being so agreeable. I expected you in my chamber last eve, arguing to stay at home."

"Nay, I accept your wisdom, Papa." She tried her best not to frown, but knew she had to tell this lie, or she would hurt her papa's feelings.

Her mama asked, "Lily, is there aught you'd like to tell us before you go?"

"Nay, all is well." Lie number three.

Aunt Gwyneth said, "You look lovely."

"My thanks. 'Tis a most lovely morn to begin a journey." She ate her porridge as she spoke.

"The sky is gray, but 'tis not raining or snowing so that makes it a good day for us." Logan moved over to the door to peek outside. "Lily, I'll see you in the stables in a few moments. Molly, Sorcha, I think 'tis time to take our leave."

Lily waited for them to go ahead of her before she moved over to kiss her mama and papa good-bye. Her mama kissed her and whispered in her ear. "You know I'll always love and support you, lass. We'll miss your smiling face here. The clan will be lost without you."

Her sire held both her hands in his. "I love you, Lilykins, no matter what. This shall be a wonderful journey for you. Please try to enjoy it."

She gave him her biggest smile, doing her best not to cry, and replied, "I know, Papa. I must be going."

Uncle Logan had taken her satchel, so she slipped on her mantle, purposefully leaving the hood down. Taking another deep breath, she opened the door and headed out.

Things were different today. No one spoke to her as she moved through the courtyard. Instead people came out to stare, their gazes never leaving her as she waved and smiled at each and every one of her clanmates.

If anyone spoke to her, she did not notice. She was too wrapped in her own thoughts and fears of what was to come. As soon as she arrived at the stables, she stepped inside the door and broke into a run, heading straight for her Tilly. As soon as she found her, she threw her arms around her dear horse and let the tears flow. "Tilly, I'm so sorry, but I cannot take you with me. Papa has decided the journey would be too difficult for you."

Tilly neighed, pawing the ground.

"I'll miss you, too, but I would not want to over work you. I'll be back soon, and I'll miss you so. Mayhap when we are in Edinburgh, I can find some ribbons for you."

Tilly nuzzled her neck.

"I know, Tilly. I cut my hair off, but 'tis not too short. It almost touches my shoulders. It has had the effect I hoped it would. None of the lads swore their love for me on the way here, and I wished to make sure none of the lads in Edinburgh would do so either. I worry Papa's goal in sending me away may be for me to find another, and you know I'll never love any lad but my Kyle. Oh, Tilly, I am so torn, and I know not what to do."

A brusque voice interrupted her from behind. "I like your hair, niece."

Lily spun around to find her uncle leaning against the door jamb, his arms crossed in front of him. "Why, many thanks, Uncle

Logan."

"It's as distinct and unique as you are, but you didn't need to do it."

"Whatever do you mean?"

"I heard what you said just now. No one will get past Kyle. He'll kill anyone who dares to look at you wrong. Now say goodbye to your horse and come along. I've chosen a nice horse for you. Sunshine…er, Tilly will be here when you return."

She gave Tilly one more kiss, and her horse pawed the ground three times. Exasperated, she huffed in indignation. "I know, Tilly. Must you keep count, too? And how could you know I lied three more times today? You were not even there to hear them."

Logan snorted as he strode down the passageway. "Lucky guess. You've been telling quite a few lately."

Lily rushed to catch up to her uncle, but as soon as she reached him, he spun around and looked at her. "And do not expect Kyle to mention your hair. Lads do not care about such things."

"But all the lads stared at me on the way here."

Logan pivoted and yelled back over his shoulder. "Lads in love do not notice these things."

Lily stopped in her tracks. Did Kyle love her?

That thought clouded her mind so much she paid little attention to her surroundings as she greeted the horse she would be riding on the journey. She rubbed the beautiful beast's neck, giving him the chance to get used to her, and whispered sweet words to him before handing him the apple she'd brought.

Kyle came up behind her. "Good morn to you, Lily. Are you ready? If so, I'll help you mount."

Lily stared at him, hoping to gauge his reaction to her shorn hair, but he barely looked at her. "Aye, I'm ready when you are."

He grabbed her by the waist and tossed her up onto her horse, where she landed with an *oof*.

"Kyle, you could have put your hands down for my foot."

"Nay, this was easier. Now remember you are to stay by my side at all times, understood?" But he did not even look at her as he said it, and he walked away as he talked.

That told her everything she needed to know about his true feelings for her and her hair.

She was ugly as an old hag.

When Torrian had first informed Kyle of his assignment, Kyle had assumed he would be traveling with Torrian, and he'd accepted the journey as part of his position. But Torrian was not going, and as the chieftain's second, his job was to stay by Torrian's side and protect him. How could he do that if he was in Edinburgh?

He'd calmed down after talking with his mother, who'd reminded him that there was no greater honor than being charged to protect a chieftain's wife or daughter. She'd advised him that the best way to make his clan proud would be to do his duty without complaint.

Then Torrian had said something else to convince him to make the journey. "If you wish to decline this assignment as Lily's guard, and I wouldn't advise that, who would you recommend I send in your place? Which warrior would protect her best without getting too close to her?"

Who, indeed? Kyle could not possibly trust any of the other warriors with the lass he loved. No one would be good enough, and he would be worried sick about her safety the whole time she was away. In fact, he was quite sure that he was entranced enough with Lily that he would have followed after the group within two or three days. Neglecting or deserting his duties would have been far worse than accepting the laird's request in the first place.

And now they were off to Edinburgh.

Uncle Logan had chosen twenty guards to go along with them. In addition, Seamus traveled with them, while Mungo stayed back to protect the castle with the rest of their guards. Kyle had to admit he was a bit anxious about this trip. He feared Logan Ramsay would discover just how distracted Lily could make him. He'd already said ten prayers for the Lord to help him focus on his duty and ignore the temptation that would be alongside him. Once mounted, he and Lily rode in the middle of the group, ten guards in front and ten at the rear.

Kyle had been told the trip might last a sennight, which meant that for a full seven nights he would be tortured by Lily's nearness without being able to touch her. Trying to control his temptation, he barely spoke to Lily initially. Even so, he noticed her somber demeanor. After a while, Kyle could no longer ignore his desire to speak to her and try to cheer her up. He attempted to talk to her on two occasions as they traveled through the forest, but she ignored him both times, seemingly deep in thought. They'd left Sunshine at home because the journey was too long for such a small horse. It disappointed him to hear Lily refer to her beloved animal as Tilly to one of her cousins. It told him that his Lily was still not her usual self.

The devil...he shook his head to jar such addled thoughts from his mind. The lass had him in a turmoil. At the end of the day, they finally chose a clearing to rest in for the night, so Kyle moved to help Lily dismount. The other guards searched the area for wildlife and reivers on Logan's instructions and then divided up their posts around the camp.

Kyle's post would be easy. He'd be at Lily's side, though he doubted she would like that at all given the tension between them. As soon as her feet hit the ground, she pushed against his chest.

"I must take care of my needs. Please be respectful, Kyle."

"I will, but do not take too long or I will come looking for you." Shite, there it was again, the aroma of flowers and the outdoors. Why did the lass have to invade his senses so?

Lily shrugged her shoulders before moving toward the creek, not waiting for her cousins or aunt to join her.

Kyle followed her, but kept a distance away. After taking care of his own needs, he moved over to the creek to wash the dirt off his hands and face. Once finished, he searched the area, but Lily was nowhere to be found. He was starting to panic when he heard sniffling off in a copse of trees, a place that was well hidden from the others.

"Lily? Are you there? Do you need help?" Kyle expected a sharp answer, but even a taste of her anger would be preferable to her sadness.

"Nay, I do not need help." Her voice was so feeble, he was sure she must be crying.

He moved toward the trees. "Lily, I'm coming in. Cover yourself."

Lily replied, "I am covered, and I've finished."

When he entered the small clearing, he saw her leaning her head and shoulders against a tree by the creek, pulling leaves off the branches and flinging them into the water.

"What's wrong, Lily?" He moved closer, though he knew it was a mistake. Every time he stood within a certain distance from her, the urge to kiss her and hold her tight drove him daft.

"Naught," she whispered, staring at the clump of leaves in her hand rather than raising her gaze to his.

"You are not the Lily I'm used to seeing." He took another step closer.

Lily dropped all the leaves she'd peeled from the trees. Even after traveling all day, she looked absolutely beautiful. Her hair was unbound, framing her face with soft waves. She had the longest eyelashes he'd ever seen on a lass, and her lips were pink and lush and delicious. He knew that from experience.

"Lily?" He pushed her to talk to him. This was not going to be a good journey if they could not even speak to each other.

"Kyle, you never noticed my hair. I must be an ugly hag, for sure."

"What about your hair? I like your hair." What could be wrong with her hair? She always kept it clean and shiny.

She held the ends up for him to see. "Did you not notice I cut it all off?"

He frowned. "Och, so you have. It does not matter to me."

Her gaze caught his and she took a step closer. "Kyle, I love you. I always have."

Kyle stared at her for a moment, unable to say anything. How long had he waited to hear those words from her lips? Aye, she'd said it to him as a wee lassie, but never as a woman. He couldn't stop himself. He took two broad strides toward her. She held her hand up and placed her palms against his chest. "Nay, not this time."

Kyle's voice, deep and husky, said, "Aye, this time. I love you and you love me. What else must we know?" In that moment it seemed so simple. He grasped her by the shoulders and tugged her toward him, covering her lips with his, sweeping his tongue inside her sweet mouth until she moaned, leaning into him, clutching his plaid in her hands.

He'd been tortured enough watching her sweet backside on the horse in front of him all day long. His arm wrapped around her waist and pulled her close. He wanted her, no, *needed* her, like he'd always needed her. But now it was different. Now he needed all of Lily.

He kissed her until she gasped and pulled back from him, staring at him with a look of surprise and delight. Encouraged, he trailed a path of smaller kisses down her neck, across the delicate bone below her chin, his tongue tasting her curves. Every part of him fought the primal urge to lay her down on the moss next to the creek and bury himself deep inside of her until she begged for more, the urge to make her his.

He loved her more than he had ever thought possible. For once, he wished to forget about responsibility and focus and stop hiding what was inside him. He and Lily were meant to be together. There were times he wished to grab her and run far away, just so they could live together on a mountain deep in the Highlands.

"Kyle," she whimpered. "Kiss me again."

He gazed into her eyes, her dazed expression urging him on. He nibbled on her bottom lip briefly until she cried out, so he pulled her close and plundered her mouth. The sensation of her crushing her body to his, pressing her breasts against him until the taut peaks threatened to burst through the material, drove him forward. He reached under her mantle and cupped her breast through the thin fabric of her gown, and she arched against him, giving him more. Her passion fueled him, and he slid one breast out of the confines of the ribbons. Kissing the side of her breast, he rubbed his thumb across her tender bud, then took her nipple in his mouth until he heard the soft cries of her surrender.

A rustling not far away stopped him. Hell, but what had he been thinking? He stopped his assault on her senses and set her a distance away, fixing the front of her gown. She stared at him, a confused expression on her face. "Kyle?"

He did not answer.

"Kyle, is it my hair?"

He gave her an irritated look. "Lily, I don't love your hair, I love you. Do as you wish with your hair."

The expression on her face bowled him over. Hellfire, she looked so damn vulnerable, he couldn't speak. Base urges roared through his veins, telling him to do as she wished him to do, what they both needed, but he fought them with all his might. A distant voice interrupted his thoughts.

"Lily?"

The voice was Molly's. "She's fine." Kyle answered. "I've got her, Molly. We'll be right there." He held his breath until he heard her retreating footsteps, then he finished tying Lily's ribbons.

"I'm sorry, Lily."

"Why?" The word was filled with all the pain of rejection.

"Because it should not have happened." He fixed her hair as best he could before he took her hand and moved out of the grouping of trees they were in.

"Why would you say such a thing? Do you not like me? This is why you break my heart, Kyle. You kiss me, then act as if you wish you'd never touched me. Do I taste foul to you?"

Kyle took a deep breath, praying for patience. He had to do his duty and his job, which meant he needed to stop the blood hurtling through him and the ache in his groin.

"Lily, I've told you how I feel. Nay, you are far from foul. The problem is that you are too sweet. But this should not be. I've taken advantage of you."

He tugged her behind him and she ran through the bushes to keep up with him.

"Why, Kyle? If we both like it, why is it wrong? I do not understand the term 'advantage.' You are always angry after you kiss me. Do you not like my kisses?"

He finally stopped and spun around, glancing around the area to make sure they would not be overheard. "Aye, Lily. I do like your kisses. You make me feel things I've never felt before, but 'tis wrong. We are not married. Your sire appointed me as your protector for this trip. I should not take advantage of the situation."

A small voice whispered to him, "But Kyle, I love you and you love me."

Logan barked out, "Maule, where the hell is my niece?"

Kyle glanced at her, tugging her forward. "Now do you understand? Your uncle would flay me a thousand ways if he'd seen us together."

Lily looked more perplexed than ever.

But what more could he possibly say?

They finally arrived in Edinburgh and Lily had to admit she was glad. Kyle had barely spoken to her after their session in the woods. She'd enjoyed every moment with him, but while Kyle had proclaimed his love for her, he'd immediately withdrawn after they rejoined the others. True, he still helped her dismount and protected her with a hawkish eye. But he did nothing beyond the duties expected of him as her guard.

She didn't know what to make of him.

Lily was standing in the hillside courtyard beside the royal castle, looking down on the view, when Molly tore over to her and grabbed her hands. "Is this not beautiful, cousin? The leaves are turning and you can see all the trees from up here. It feels as if we are in the heavens staring down at the world. I love Edinburgh, especially the way the keep sits so majestically atop the hill. Are you not truly glad to be here?"

Sorcha joined them. "Aye, 'tis glorious here, Molly. I cannot wait to meet all the lads in Edinburgh." Her giggling cut off when Kyle joined them.

He fell in at Lily's side, and together they all waited for Logan and Gwyneth to return from the castle. Lily hated it when he stood so close that she had to breathe in his scent. Why must he torture her so? How could he kiss her like she was the only lass in the world for him and then act like it had never happened?

Logan and Gwyneth emerged a short while later, and they ushered them inside. As soon as they stepped into the corridor, a maid greeted them. Gwyneth said, "She's here to show us to our rooms, lasses. Kyle, you may come along and wait outside while we unpack. Logan, we shall return shortly while you meet with King Alexander."

Lily dragged her feet as she followed her cousins up the stairs. While they chattered as cheerfully as two wee birds, Kyle and Lily did not speak at all. She peeked at him once, but he stared straight ahead. When they arrived at their chamber, her cousins stepped inside and gasped.

"Lily, 'tis most beautiful, do you not agree?" Sorcha spun about in a circle. The bed in the center of the chamber was large enough for all the three of them, and there was also a large hearth with four chairs and a table in front of it. Mounds and mounds of pillows and furs decorated the bed, and lovely tapestries graced the walls. A side table sat on either side of the bed.

Kyle bowed to Lily and said, "I'll await you outside the door."

As soon as he left, Sorcha grabbed her hand and said, "What is wrong, Lily? I've not seen you so sad!"

Rather than answer her, Lily set to unpacking her satchel.

Gwyneth rested her hand on her shoulder, and said, "Lily did not wish to come as you did, Sorcha. We must be patient with her."

"And Kyle is being a fool. He hardly ever speaks to her." Molly huffed as she spun around to set some of her things on one of the side tables.

Lily finished with her satchel and sat on a chair in front of the hearth, taking in the warmth of the fire. She sat for a long time, staring at the crackling flames while her family finished their chores. Though she hoped to find some answer about Kyle, the peace she sought did not come. There were only more questions. A short while later, they all headed down to the great hall for a small afternoon meal.

Her cousins had done their best to cheer her up, but to no avail. No matter how she tried, she could not laugh and act as if the situation did not trouble her. Their king had insisted they stay at the royal castle, replete with its many comforts, but she soon slipped out to tend to her horse, wanting to be alone, and she managed to escape while Kyle spoke to Logan. She missed Tilly so.

"My lady, I have groomed your beautiful horse for you," the stable lad said, giving a small bow.

She smiled gaily at him. "Thank you for your kindness. You did a fine job. He looks quite handsome." She strode past him and headed into her horse's stall, closing the door behind her so no one would hear her conversation with her horse. Wrapping her arms around her horse's neck, she whispered, "Why does he not do as he says? He says he loves me, but he does not act as if he has any feelings at all."

A loud voice echoed down the corridor. "Lily? Will you stop trying to evade me?" Kyle flung the door open moments later and glowered at her. "Why must you sneak away?"

Lily pursed her lips and turned to face him. "Because my heart does not sing when I'm with you, Kyle Maule."

He ran his hand down his face. A range of emotions crossed it before he opened his mouth, but she never did find out what he would have said. He was interrupted by her uncle, who had come up behind him.

"Lily?" Uncle Logan asked. "We're walking to the fair in town. Would you like to come along?"

"Aye, I would love to go with you to the fair." She turned to Kyle. "You need not come. I'm sure Torrian would trust me with my aunt and uncle to keep me company. Mayhap you should spend some time on your own, clear your head of all that clutters it. I believe 'twould be helpful for you to know your own mind better." Not able to stop herself, she set her hand on his strong forearm as she moved past him to follow her uncle back down the corridor.

Kyle caught up with her. "I'll not allow you to go without me."

She spoke over her shoulder to him, not changing her stride. "I believe you'd like your freedom, so I am giving it to you. You are now free of me for a short time."

Kyle's feet did not slow. "The only one who can relieve me of my duties is your chieftain and brother, and since he's not here, I'll continue with the task he assigned to me."

The man followed her so closely that she could feel his heat. What the devil did she need to do to get him to keep his distance? Did he not know how his presence tortured her? She closed her eyes in frustration. Just looking at the man hurt her, causing strange lumps to form all over her insides: her throat, her heart, her belly, her head. How she wished he'd just leave her be. If he did not want to act on their feelings for each other, he should give her space. "Uncle Logan, would you please relieve Kyle of his duties?"

Once they stepped outside of the stables, Logan stopped and waited for Lily and Kyle to catch up to him. "Nay, I'll not do that. 'Tis his job to protect you, which means he'll go where ever you go. And if I ever see him away from you, he'll have to answer to me. He's to come with us."

"Uncle Logan, please? He deserves some time alone."

Logan tipped his head toward Lily. "Since when does my niece whine so? I've not heard you whine before. What brings this out of you?" Logan's hands settled on his hips.

"I know not of what you speak, Uncle. I'm not whining." Lily folded her hands in front of her, giving Kyle her back. "Why, I'm quite happy to be going to the fair with you, Uncle Logan."

Logan's gaze narrowed. "Good, keep it that way. I was afraid someone had switched my niece with a wee gremlin. Whoever thinks to do such a horrid thing shall have to deal with me. I love my Lily—the happy, sweet, smiling Lily, not the whining sad one." Then he leaned over and hugged her so tight she could barely breathe. "My sweet niece, forgive me. I know 'tis a difficult time for you, especially since your sire forced this trip on you, but we must make the best of it. I'll find a way to bring back that beautiful smile of yours. I know you're not happy to be here, but I'm thrilled to have you along."

"Forgive me. I'll try my best." She plastered a smile on her face and vowed not to remove it. Since Kyle would be right next to her, this would truly serve as a challenge for her. "Please, may we go now?"

They made their way to the front of the castle, where they met up with Sorcha, Molly, and Gwyneth. Lily took a moment to take in the sight in front of her. Edinburgh Castle sat high on a hill, so high that one could see almost all the vendors and buildings in the entire burgh. The plethora of colors and the sweet aroma of pine trees caused her to lift her face to the winds, taking in the glory of the outdoors.

"I love this view most of all. Do you not agree?" Molly came up beside her. "I love Edinburgh. I'm sorry you do not like it, but I could be happy living here. Maggie hates it and swears she'll never visit again."

A few moments later, Aunt Gwyneth joined them. "'Tis a lovely day for a walk, do you not agree, Lily?"

Squeezing her forced smile a little wider, Lily answered, "Of course, 'tis a glorious day, and I look forward to the fair. Might we stop at the merchants' booths?"

"What would you like to see?" Molly asked.

"Aunt Gwyneth, would you take us to the booth that carried that beautiful selection of ribbons, please?"

Off they headed toward the center of the burgh. Lily found her mood brightening as they passed the first of the bustling booths, the sight of the many vendors and the townspeople making her forget her confusing feelings for the lad next to her.

Aunt Gwyneth stopped to check a supply of sharp-looking daggers, then lingered near a booth with the nicest boots Lily had ever seen. Logan leaped forward and picked out a pair for his wife and for both of his daughters, choosing a similar pair for Maggie.

"Lily, would you like to choose a pair of boots, too?"

"Nay. Those are not my type, Uncle, but thank you for thinking of me."

The more colorful flags and banners she saw, the better she felt. She started to hum a tune she often hummed to her horse as she moved from vendor to vendor to see all the wares. She watched young lovers at the floral booth, the men choosing bouquets for their loves and delighting in the smiles brought by the flowers. There were colorful silks waving in the wind, woolen materials for gowns, embroidery threads. Logan swept over in a flash to grab a scarf for Gwyneth, and she kissed him when he presented it to her. "The green reminds me of the forest, your favorite place, Gwynie."

Kyle bought nothing, and his attention was focused solely on Lily and every lad who walked by her. The closer the lads came to her, the closer Kyle hovered. At one point, a lad almost brushed her arm. Kyle was there in an instant, shoving him away from Lily, glowering at him as he pushed.

Once Kyle pushed the lad away, Lily whispered through gritted teeth, "Must you, Kyle? You look at every lad as if they are about to steal me, and none have approached me at all."

"I know you are not worried, but I am. 'Tis my job, and I'll do it as I see fit. They need to keep their distance. He came too close to you with a look in his eyes I did not like."

"If you must, but please do not hurt anyone or cause any fights. I'd like to enjoy the fair."

Kyle grumbled, but she couldn't understand him, so she continued on, gazing at all the wares available.

"There it is," Sorcha shouted in excitement. "The ribbon booth. 'Tis up ahead, Lily."

Lily caught sight of the booth and took off, only to find herself yanked back by a pair of strong arms.

"Lily, please do not leave my side. There are many strangers here. You must be careful."

"Kyle, I was only going to the booth up ahead."

"I'll go with you."

She almost hung her head, tired of being yelled at, but then she thought of Uncle Logan's previous comment about her whining, so she jerked her head back up and plastered a sweet smile on her face. "Then please lead the way, Kyle."

"Aye, lead the way, Kyle," Logan said, his voice gruff. "And while she's looking at her ribbons, you and I need to talk."

CHAPTER ELEVEN

The lass would surely be the death of him. How many lads had stared at her beauty as they passed her? He did his best to stare them all down, but most of them were so lost in Lily's aura they didn't even notice he was there. He wanted to growl at every male who passed her.

This was the worst assignment he'd ever had. How was one supposed to protect the most beautiful woman in the world? Torrian had given him an impossible task. He sighed to himself as he led Lily toward the ribbon booth.

Logan pulled him back while Lily moved around the booth to look at the large variety of ribbons. There was a joyous smile on her face that was not one bit fake this time.

"Lad, if you wish to make a lass happy," Logan murmured, "you should think of buying her a gift."

"My apologies, my lord, but I'm not here to buy her gifts. I'm here to protect her, and as you can see, 'tis a difficult job at times. She does not pay attention to her surroundings."

Gwyneth slipped in next to Logan while her lasses joined Lily's delighted examination of the velvet ribbons and silks. "I overheard your last comment," she said to Kyle. "Nay, she does not, and that is part of what makes Lily so special. She lives in a world that I could only wish to share with her, and I choose to do so as much as I can."

"I do not understand." Kyle was more confused than ever.

"Lily has a unique view of the world," Logan said, taking Gwyneth's hand, "and 'tis why she's so special. Seems to me 'tis part of the reason you love her as much as we do."

Kyle opened his mouth to argue, but Logan held his hand up to stop him.

"Lad, we know you love her, so there's no point in denying it to us. You must stop denying it to yourself. Aye, she's carefree and needs watching, but you need not destroy the verra things that make her joyful inside. Have you not seen how happy she is around the ribbons, the colors, the excitement? Lily's different, and you know it. She's even different with animals. I swear Sunshine speaks her language. We understand your need to protect her, but you must do it without crushing her."

Kyle nodded, and Gwyneth and Logan headed into the booth to oh and ah over the lasses' findings. He knew they were right about Lily. It *was* one of the reasons he loved her. What was it she'd told him when she was but a wee one? A hug makes your day better. She'd been absolutely right about that. The lass had the sweetest outlook of anyone he'd ever known, and a hug from her could set any day straight. She could make anyone's heart sing, but not lately, and he knew he was to blame.

He'd crushed her spirit in the woods. She was an innocent, so she hadn't understood why he would stop kissing her abruptly, without explanation. In all likelihood, she didn't understand what he'd almost done, what he'd wished to do more than anything. He recalled the look of confusion on her dazed face the day he'd discovered her inside the cottage with a nude Ranulf and Davina. Sweat broke out across his forehead as the thought of Logan catching him on top of Lily made its way into his mind. He'd be hung by his ballocks for sure—if he had any left when Logan and Gwyneth finished with him. And he'd deserve it.

Lily's laughter caught his attention, along with everyone else in the area. She was holding up three brightly colored ribbons, braiding them together to see if they were the shades she wanted. She giggled and hummed, and sure enough, lads started to gather around the stall like flies around honey. They stood watching as Lily caressed the ribbons and giggled with her cousins.

And Kyle moved to protect her, pushing his way through the gawking bystanders so he was directly behind her. Unfortunately, one of the lads he had pushed aside shoved him back, causing him to fall into Lily. He almost knocked her over, and dozens of ribbons went flying into the air.

Chaos ensued. Kyle turned around and punched the offender in the nose, sending him flailing backwards into the crowd. That set off another two lads, who headed straight for Kyle with their fists pulled back, intent on damaging everything in their path.

Kyle picked the two lads up and tossed them to the other side of the path, growling at them to stay back. Logan pulled his sword out of his sheath, so Kyle did the same.

The crowd backed away from the two Highlanders ready to thrust their swords at the next fool to challenge them, but then Kyle noticed something that made him forget about everything—and everyone—else. From the corner of his eye, he saw Lily running haphazardly in the opposite direction. He yelled her name, but she continued to run, the crowd growing thicker and thicker all around her.

Logan yelled, "Go after her, my lasses are all here."

Kyle sheathed his sword and chased after Lily, winding in and out of strangers, his heart now in his throat because he was losing sight of her. She continued to run, as if in some sort of panic, oblivious to everything around her. As she took off around a bend in the path, he sped up, shoving bystanders out of his way. "Move, please, I must catch her. Out of my way!"

His heart was in his throat, but when he finally made it around the bend, she was nowhere to be seen. He charged ahead, yelling at the crowd to allow him through. Some people were actually wise enough to get out of his way just because of his size; others were pushed aside by his mad dash.

Hellfire, where was she? He did not even know which direction to take.

A scream ripped through the din of the crowd, and he was sure it was Lily's. His heart thudded, threatening to burst out of his chest, as he ran toward the sound. To his surprise, she was headed straight for him, yelling his name.

"Kyle, Kyle! Help me, Kyle. He's here. I heard him!" Her arms flailed in a panic, so he moved toward her as fast as he could.

When she finally reached him, she launched herself straight at him and he caught her in midair, her arms wrapping around his neck in a grip that told him she never wanted to let go.

He hugged her tight, then whispered in her ear, "Are you all right? Is aught wrong?"

She pulled back, her tear-stained face full of fear. She cupped his face and said, "My thanks for following me. 'Twas him. I'm sure of it."

"Lily, my sweet Lily, slow down." He headed over to the side of the fair, searching for a quiet area for them to sit down, away from the stares of the crowd just now dispersing. He found a bench and sat, settling her on his lap. "What is it? What happened?"

"Oh, Kyle, I was running because of all the fighting. I know I shouldn't have, but I hate to watch you and Uncle Logan fight. I'm always so afraid you'll get hurt." Her breath hitched a few times before she could continue.

She let her hands drop and grabbed his arms as if she were afraid to let him go. "I was running back toward the castle, but someone grabbed me. He said he loved me and told me to stop."

He kissed her forehead, then wiped her tears away. "Did you get a better look at him this time?"

"Nay. He grabbed me from behind, and I screamed and ran away. There were two or three men behind me, and he could have been any of them. I think he had brown hair, but 'tis all I know. Again, all I saw was his hair." Sobbing again, she buried her face in his shoulder.

He scooped her in his arms and carried her toward the castle. "I'm taking you back. We'll get your ribbons another day. The fair will be here for a while."

Lily wrapped her arms tight around his neck. "Nay, I'm never leaving home again, and I do not want to come back to the fair. Kyle, promise me you'll never leave me. Please? What would I do without you?"

"Lily, I'll never leave you. You should know that by now. I'll protect you forever." He kissed her cheek again, and she nuzzled his neck as he carried her toward the castle.

"I know, Kyle. I know you'll protect me. Please do not ever stop loving me."

"Lily, I'll love you forever. Do you not realize that yet?"

By the time he reached the castle, she was sound asleep in his arms.

Kyle had brought her back to the chamber she was sharing with Sorcha and Molly, and she'd slept a short time before Aunt Gwyneth had come in to ask her about the incident at the fair.

"Lily, how do you fare?" Her aunt brushed her short curls with her fingers, trying to straighten out the mess.

"I am better, Aunt. I am hungry, may we find something to eat? Forgive me for sleeping so long."

"I think your mind needed the rest. This has been a difficult journey for you, and I am sorry for all you have had to deal with. Come with Molly and Sorcha and me, we'll eat together."

The king had arranged for them to take their midday meal alone in a small chamber because of the circumstances, for which Lily was extremely grateful. The last thing she wanted was to be around strangers. Aunt Gwyneth helped her get ready to greet the others before stepping into the passageway.

Kyle was waiting outside their chamber when she opened the door, and he escorted them downstairs for the meal with her family. She was so glad to see him that she latched onto him as soon as she saw him. He settled her down on the bench, but before he could move away from her, she tugged him down next to her, clinging to his arm. Everyone was present except for Logan, who was in a meeting with the king.

She could not help it. Others thought she was daft, but she knew what she'd heard. "Kyle, please stay by my side this eve? Please?"

He took her hand in his and whispered, "I'll not leave you, Lily. He'll not get to you. You're in the royal castle with your aunt and uncle and me to protect you. Do not worry."

There was the sound of approaching footsteps, and then her uncle's booming voice brought her attention back to the table. "Lily, tell me again about this man, the one who attacked you."

She glanced at her family gathered around her, comforted by their presence and their concern. They would protect her, she had to believe in them. Between the king's guards and the Ramsay guards, there were more in and around the royal castle than she could count. "Uncle Logan, he did not attack me. He grabbed my hand and tugged at me."

"Did you wish to go with him?" Her uncle paced a short path in front of her.

"Nay, of course not." Shocked at her uncle's suggestion, she squeezed Kyle's hand. "But he has never hurt me. Both times I saw him, he just asked me to go with him."

"If he's going against your wishes, he's attacking you. Do not look at it any other way, Lily," Uncle Logan stopped in front of her and bent down to address her. When he continued, his voice was softer, as if he understood the depths of her fear. "Lads are not above the use of trickery with a lass. They'll be nice and sweet while taking you hostage. Never give them the opportunity. Any time someone tries to make you do something you do not wish to do, 'tis an attack against you, no matter how friendly they may seem."

"Aye, Uncle. I'll remember."

"He probably wishes for you to marry him," Molly said.

Lily gasped, staring at her cousin. "He cannot. Nay, I would never marry a stranger."

"I'm thinking you've met him before," Gwyneth said. "He's not of our clan or you would have recognized him. Are you sure there is naught familiar about him?"

Lily stared at her lap, closing her eyes to recall everything she could of the lad, but naught came to her. "Nay, I saw naught."

Logan asked, "His voice? Does it not sound familiar?"

"Nay," Lily whispered. She leaned her head against Kyle's shoulder. "When can we leave, Uncle? I wish my father had never sent me here."

"Unfortunately, we will not be leaving just yet. I'll pose a question to you, and I'll leave the decision entirely up to you because I realize how upset you are. I've already spoken to King Alexander about this matter. He has asked us—meaning me, Gwyneth, Molly, and Sorcha—to travel to the Buchans. He fears more trouble from them since Glenn has not accepted his son's death or his guilt in the situation with Heather. We will be leaving shortly."

Lily jerked backwards, and would have knocked herself off the back of the bench had Kyle not reached out to catch her. "Nay, nay, I'll not go. Please, Uncle Logan. I..."

Logan held his hand up. "You have the king's permission to stay here in the castle while we are gone. I trust Kyle to protect you, and I'll leave several guards with him to do as he sees fit. You do not need to step outside. I can arrange for the maids to serve you in your chamber, if you would prefer, or you can eat in the great hall with the others. There will be entertainment tonight and on the morrow, and the king assured me he will have many guards there. Mayhap it would be best for you to be around others. No one would try to kidnap you from the middle of the royal hall with so many witnesses. When you are above stairs, Kyle will stand guard outside your door and he'll post guards in whatever passageways he deems appropriate. The king is allowing our men to guard you along with the royal guards."

Lily leaned closer to Kyle. "Aye, my thanks, Uncle. I would prefer to await you here." Tears welled in her eyes, but she fought to keep them at bay. They did not understand how unsettled she was to be away from home, away from her sire and brother and Mama. And now she knew that horrid man had followed her... Well, she'd have to deal with it, and she'd have to depend on Kyle.

And with just the two of them together, he'd be angry with her again for certain.

Kyle was inwardly grateful that Lily had chosen not to go to the Buchans. The thought of protecting her in those surroundings made his insides boil. He recalled every moment he had spent there with Torrian during his friend's short and ill-fated betrothal to Davina of Buchan. The keep had been overrun with men, full of unsavory characters who would toss any lass down for their own satisfaction. It was the type of castle where the men controlled everything, with nary a female touch anywhere.

The Buchans and the MacNivens had planned to take over the Highlands, and they'd started with the Ramsays by arranging a betrothal between Davina and Torrian. But their plan had been uncovered, and they'd lost the Buchan heir in an ill-fated attack on the Ramsays. The MacNiven chieftain, Ranulf, had been tried and found guilty of treason for going against the king's direct order. The king had sentenced him to death by hanging. There were only three Buchans left: Chief Glenn, his daughter Davina, and his youngest son Cormag.

The Buchan castle would not be a friendly environment, and Kyle was grateful everyone had agreed Lily needed to stay at the royal burgh. It surprised him a little that Logan would take his daughters into such an environment. He could only guess that he was doing so at the king's request.

Nay, if Kyle had his way, Lily Ramsay would never again step foot near the Buchans.

Logan pulled him away from the chamber to speak to him before he left. "Lad, I do not worry about you protecting my niece. I've seen you in action twice now, but I feel the need to remind you that you refused a betrothal to my niece. Please keep that in the back of your mind. You'll treat her respectfully, as you have always done. Do you understand my meaning?"

Kyle nodded, unable to speak. Aye, he knew exactly what Logan Ramsay meant—and what consequences he would face should he lose control of himself.

"My lord, are you sure you wish to take Sorcha and Molly to the Buchans?" Perhaps he shouldn't ask, but he was concerned.

"Gwynie guards Molly, who is quite capable on her own, and I guard Sorcha. You guard Lily. 'Tis the only safe way to do it. I'll take many guards and leave several with you. I'm trusting you. Is there aught you need before we take our leave?"

"Aye, there is one boon I would ask of you, if you do not mind."

"Whatever you need, I'll see to it, then we'll be on our way. I expect to return to the castle in two or three days. I'll have one of the king's stewards check on you each day, and as I said, I'll leave several guards here with you. Trust me, we shall not tarry. This is an unexpected part of our journey and I do not look forward to it."

Kyle gave Logan the list of things he needed, then thanked him and moved back inside the chamber. He prayed for strength before he stepped inside.

He was about to be left alone with the lass he loved…at a time when she was extremely vulnerable.

How in hell was he to survive such a challenge?

CHAPTER TWELVE

Lily had been pacing her chamber for hours. How could she possibly be expected to sleep alone after what happened at the fair? She twisted her hands in the folds of her night rail, moving over to the small window in her chamber before she pulled the fur back to stare outside. She'd heard a noise, of that she was certain, but what was it? The moon shone brightly at her, casting a shadow in the room, something she usually enjoyed.

Suddenly lost in the sight of the night moon, she held back the fur so the moonlight would fall upon her bed, smiling at the faerie dust fluttering around her. It may only have been in her imagination, but it made her feel better nonetheless. After Lily had been kidnapped and nearly killed years and years ago, her mama had spent many nights in her bed with her. And every time there was a full moon, Mama had told her the faeries danced across her chamber in the moonlight, spreading their magic dust to protect her. According to Mama, the dust could only be seen by those who were quiet and observant.

Mama had even taught her to sing with the faeries, and Lily had done so nearly every full moon since then. Sighing, she tipped her head back to allow the light of the moon to fall across her face, as if the light could cast magic across her features. How she'd often wished it would warm her face like the beams of the sun, but her stepmother had taught her that moonbeams were special and unique and worthy of being cherished as such.

Another sound startled her, this time from the passageway. Hell, but she hadn't thought about the fact that she'd be sleeping alone until her family returned. This big bed had held Lily, Sorcha, and Molly with no problem. Even at home, once Bethia had come along years and years ago, she'd always had someone to share her bed. This giant bed was empty, and she was lost in the middle of it.

Another bang echoed through the chamber, and she bolted over to the door and flung it open so fast that Kyle fell backward into her room.

Kyle leaped to his feet, his hand already on the hilt of his sword. "Lily? What's wrong?"

She sighed as the sight of her true love washed over her, comforting her in ways she'd never admit. "My apologies, Kyle. I heard a noise, and I thought something might have happened to you."

He brushed the dirt from the floor off his plaid. "Lily, I told you I'd be here guarding your door all night, but I must lean against it to sleep. Could you not open it a bit more gingerly next time?" He rubbed the back of his head. "The guard at the end of the passageway dropped his goblet."

"Kyle, forgive me. I'm unsettled. I miss Sorcha and Molly."

Kyle wrapped his arms around her and rested his chin on the top of her head. "Lily, I know you're unsettled, but can you not trust that I'll protect you? You'll hear other sounds I will not be able to identify."

She breathed in his scent, closing her eyes in the hopes she could bring his comforting aroma back to bed with her.

Kyle edged her back toward the bed, tucked her under the covers, and gave her a quick kiss on her forehead.

"Kyle?" She rolled onto her side so she was facing him.

"Lily," he said, breathing out the loudest sigh she'd ever heard. "If I am inside the room, I'll not be able to protect you. You would distract me from my purpose, and I know you do not want that."

She frowned at him. "Aye, you've told me that a few times already tonight."

"Lass, close your eyes and go to sleep. 'Twill be morning before you know it."

He gave her a chaste kiss on the lips before returning to the passageway.

She rolled onto her back and wiggled her toes in the thick furs, trying to keep Kyle's scent fresh in her mind as she focused on the warmth of his lips on her skin. Something niggled at the back of her mind, something bad, but she tried her best to ignore it. She glanced up at the wooden beams over her head, and in the dark of the night, all she could envision were tree branches, hordes and hordes of thick tree branches in the night, the dense green leaves blocking both the sun and the moon. It looked just like the tree she'd been tied to all those years ago.

And she fell fast asleep, tree branches foremost in her mind...

Lily was back in the forest running. She ran until her legs hurt, but then a face jumped out at her.

Iona. The mean woman who had hurt her when she was a wee one cackled at her. The foolish woman thought she could hurt Lily again, but she wouldn't allow any such thing.

Lily spun around and ran in the opposite direction. "Go away, Iona. You are dead." She tore into the forest where the trees were dense, where the sun didn't shine and the moonbeams were rarely seen, but she did not stop. Iona would never touch her again.

A voice called out to her, laughing. Iona continued to follow her, crashing through the bushes fast on her tail. "You think you can get away, but you cannot. Do you know why, Miss Lily?"

Tears welled in Lily's eyes, pouring down her cheeks as Iona continued to taunt her.

"Lily, they're all going to leave you just as I left you in that tree. Can you not see what is to come? Your mother left you first, then Growley. Now Torrian has left you for his wife. They do not care about you any longer."

"Go away, Iona. I hate you!" she screamed, but Iona continued to taunt her.

"You know I'm right, 'tis why you run. They shall all leave you. They do not need wee Lily. What do you do for them? You are not a healer, not a laird's wife. You are naught to them."

"Be quiet, Iona. They love me, and 'tis all that matters." Tears spilled onto her cheeks as she ran past tree branches that tore into her tender skin, but she knew not where to go. Iona was right. She'd been deserted by everyone.

She tripped over a branch and fell face first onto the ground. Placing her hands underneath her, she tried to push herself up from the ground but found she could not. Both of her hands were tied to a tree. But how could that be?

"Gwyneth will not find you this time, Lily." Iona's face

appeared below her, her eyes lit with evil, chortling with delight over her fate. "The visit to the Buchans was a ruse to get away from you. You've become a burden to your loved ones."

Long ago Iona had bound her to a tree and left her there. It couldn't be...could it? But aye, the ground crumbled beneath her and she lay atop an old piece of wood, teetering on a tree branch. It was exactly what had happened to her when she was a wee bairn.

Shivering, she looked down at the vast tree trunk.

A treetop pushed up through the ground as if with evil intent, ripping and shredding everything in its path, catching Lily's board and heaving it higher into the air, higher and higher.

"No one will ever find you." Iona's laughing face shrunk as Lily was catapulted to the top of the thick green forest. "They've all left you."

The tree moved up and up as if it were a giant stalk of beans, and vines snaked around her legs, threatening to attach her to the tree.

"Torrian's left you, and your papa sent you away."

Lily kicked and kicked at the vines to get them off of her. A loud scream echoed behind her.

"Uncle Logan and Aunt Gwyneth and your cousins could not wait to leave you here alone. They're praying for that strange man to steal you away."

Another vine wrapped around Lily's leg, threatening to yank her off the board. She would die for sure. The cold greenery coiled around her ankle, then up toward her knee. She kicked to loosen it, but soon as it stopped moving up her leg, another vine wrapped around her other leg, writhing and coiling up the skin of her calf like a cold snake. The end of the vine felt like the viper's tongue against her skin.

The screaming stopped for just a moment as she looked at the ground and the branches and the vines, all swirling beneath her, all headed directly toward her.

"And now Kyle's left you, too. He abandoned his post as soon as you fell asleep. You're all alone. Forever."

Suddenly one of the vines peered at her with a snake's eyes, and a forked tongue shot out toward her lips.

The screaming started again, getting louder and louder until she realized something.

The screaming was coming from her.

Kyle had never heard anyone scream the way Lily was screaming, and the sound shot fear straight to his heart. "Lily," he said, shaking her gently. "Lily, wake up. Shhhhh. You'll wake the entire castle. Hush, sweets."

Lily bolted up in bed, staring at Kyle as if she had no idea where she was. The next moment, she launched herself at him, knocking him over on the bed until she lay on top of him.

"Kyle, thank you for saving me." Her cheeks were still wet with tears.

"Saving you? Lily, naught happened to you. You were having a bad dream."

She sat up and crossed her legs in front of her, her breathing so rapid that Kyle was sure she'd had the fright of her life. Her eyes blinked repeatedly until she finally focused on his face.

He pushed himself to a sitting position before cocooning her cold hands inside his warm ones. "Lily. 'Tis all right. Naught has happened."

She stared at him. "Kyle, my dream was awful. Please do not leave me."

"I will not leave you until you are settled again."

She brought herself up to her knees, her hands grasping his shoulders, "Nay, you must promise me. Promise me you will not leave me tonight." She shook his shoulders. "Promise me you'll *never* leave me. You do not understand. Everyone left me, everyone. Mama, Torrian and my papa, and Aunt Gwyneth and Uncle Logan, Sorcha, Molly, my sisters. Everyone."

"I'll not leave you." He placed his fingers under her chin, forcing her to look at him.

Fresh tears splashed down her cheeks. "But you did. In my dream, you left too, Kyle. I was all alone, and the vines on the trees turned into snakes, and they came for me…"

Kyle pulled her toward him, settling her onto his lap. "Lily, 'twas a dream, naught more. Your aunt and uncle and cousins will return. I'll not leave you. I'll be right outside your door."

"Nay," she shouted as she gripped his plaid. "Not outside my door. You must stay here, with me, in this chamber. *Please*, Kyle." She brushed the tears away. "Please stay with me."

Hellfire, but how could he turn her down? She looked completely broken. He didn't have the heart to push her away from him.

"All right. But I must let you go for a moment." He climbed out of bed to move toward the door, and the fear on her face wrenched his soul. He stepped outside to speak with his guards. When he returned, he said, "Lily, I'm right here. I'm just putting some extra protection in place."

Her loud screaming had changed to quiet sobs, and he couldn't decide which reaction was worse. He shoved a chest in front of the door after he bolted it, just in case anyone tried to bother them.

Removing his boots, his breeches, and his sword—though he was careful to make sure it was within an arm's reach—Kyle climbed onto the bed, resting his head on the pillow and holding his arms out to Lily.

She smiled and fell in next to him, whispering, "My thanks, Kyle. I could not bear it if I lost you." She nuzzled her head against his shoulder and closed her eyes.

"Do you wish to tell me more about your dream?" he whispered, caressing her back with rhythmic feathering strokes, hoping to calm her. Her heart still raced, and her breathing needed to slow a bit more. What else could he do for her?

"Iona, 'twas about Iona and the tree branches and the dark and snakes, and all the while she laughed at me, telling me no one cared about me, that I'd be alone forever." She snuggled against his chest.

Kyle recalled the time when Lily had gone missing. Logan had just returned to introduce his betrothed Gwyneth to the clan. Torrian had felt so guilty for failing to stop that daft woman from stealing his sister, but he'd still been weak from his childhood illness. It was Gwyneth who'd found Lily up in the trees, too sickly to move. According to the tales, Lily and Gwyneth had both been near death when they were found. He'd heard Logan Ramsay tell the story once, and merely listening to it had made him seethe with rage.

"And you know 'tis all false, aye?"

"Aye, but 'twas so real."

Lily tucked herself even closer to him, and he swore if she moved any closer, his erection would scare her right out of the bed.

He stared at the ceiling, trying to come up with any thoughts other than the soft warmth of his sweet lass next to him, the pressure of her breasts causing a sweat to break out across his forehead.

Logan Ramsay. That's what he needed to think about, Logan Ramsay standing in the doorway with his sword drawn.

Lily pushed up on her elbows, her hand grasping his chin to turn his gaze to hers. "Kyle, kiss me again. 'Tis the only thing that will help me forget."

"There's naught I'd rather do, lass, but…" He cut himself off with a growl, lifting up on his elbows and turning her beneath him. He kissed her tenderly at first, his hands cupping her face, not wishing to startle her because she was so vulnerable at this moment. Promising himself he would not take advantage of her, he pulled back to suckle her lower lip, only to be surprised by the tentative touch of her tongue to his.

That one movement somehow managed to knock down every barrier he had in place. Hellfire, but she was so beautiful and loving and warm. Capturing her lips with his, he slanted his mouth over hers, tasting her, teasing her until she cried out, just enough to put him completely over the edge of any sensibility.

He was lost in all that was Lily. He knew it, but he no longer cared. All his carefully contained control, everything he'd done to battle his need to be with Lily, had just fled him, leaving him with naught but a lust that could not be sated. Hellfire, he wanted Lily more than he'd ever wanted any lass.

He kissed a trail down her neck and across the fine bone in front of her chest to the valley of her breasts. To his astonishment, she clutched his upper arms and said, "Aye, Kyle. 'Tis what I want, you and only you."

"Lily, my sweet precious Lily. Do you know how often I've dreamed of this, of tasting every inch of you? You make me wild with desire."

"Aye! More! I want all of you. Do you not know we were meant to be together? 'Tis our destiny. You understand?" Her innocent gaze caught his and he groaned, taking her lips in his again. She ended the kiss abruptly and pushed him away so she could sit up.

Tearing at her ribbons, she unlaced them and lifted her gown over her head, then tossed it off to the side. He was frozen, unable to move, unmanned by her innocence, her trust in him. She had given herself over completely to her emotions, a move that humbled him.

Lily, his beautiful Lily lay on the bed in front of him, her chemise tossed to the side in haste. She lifted her chin to him, a beautiful smile dancing across her face. "Can you not feel it, Kyle?" She lifted her arms over her head in wild abandon. "This is how 'tis meant to be between us. Love me, taste me, so I can do the same to you. Show me your true desire."

Kyle stared at Lily, the most beautiful lass he'd ever seen, her skin glowing with a fine sheen that he needed to taste. He tossed his clothing off and leaned in to nuzzle her neck, cupping her breasts in his hands, his desire overtaking his reason. "Lily, my Lily, do you have any idea how beautiful you are?"

She smiled, running her hands across the muscles in his arms. "Make me yours, Kyle. I can feel how right it is for us to be together. Show me everything. Show me what love is about, how it feels to be one with another. Show me."

He knew he should stop, but he could not. Instead, he lowered his lips to her breast, nibbling and suckling each sensitive apex until she cried out and dug her nails into his shoulder. Her passionate response to him fueled him forward, all the pent-up desire for her after all these moons finally sparking to life.

A small part of him knew it was all wrong, but his heart knew it was all right. This was meant to be, Lily in his arms forever, her body sizzling with desire, and his body fevered with a need to be one with her.

"Lily, we should stop," he forced himself to say after lifting his head from the valley of her creamy flesh, caressing and molding her sweetly curved mounds in his hands. "I swear you have the softest skin ever. But we must stop."

"Never, Kyle, Never."

CHAPTER THIRTEEN

Never, she would never stop this beautiful thing arcing between them. Her body thrummed in response to his touch, but she needed to touch him the way he was touching her. His soft caress stirred a need inside of her belly that she did not understand, but she wished to do the same for him.

"Kyle, please. I wish to feel your skin."

His gaze almost made her afraid of what he would say, but he gave her a wicked grin after a moment and rolled onto his back. "I'm all yours, lass."

Lily rose up on her knees and positioned herself next to him, her hands trembling as she sat back and moved them to his skin. She locked gazes with him and started with her thumb, running it across his lower lip. He growled and suckled her thumb until a craving grew deep inside her belly. She pulled her hand away and shook her head at him. "Kyle, 'tis my turn. I wish to know all of you."

Her hands followed a path of their own, traveling down each shoulder, across the rippling muscles in his upper arms and then spanning his chiseled chest before settling one finger on each nipple. She brushed her thumbs across him, emboldened by the response she received from the man she loved. His entire body tensed at her torture, so she massaged his chest, the tough muscles flexing in front of her before she moved on to his hard belly, caressing him, teasing him with delight.

"Kyle, your manly parts move on their own, do they not?" She giggled as she teased him with the tip of her finger, following the line of coarse hairs down the middle of his abdomen and finally moving on to his jutting manhood. "You are so hard, yet the skin is so soft. I wonder how it will feel to have you inside of me."

"Lily, I cannot."

"Aye, Kyle. I want you inside of me. Make me yours." Her fingers caressed a circle around the tip of his penis, before running down the length of him, stroking his turgid arousal. She experimented with different pressures on his hardness to see how he reacted, pleased whenever he arched his pelvis toward her in response to her playful touch.

He bolted up as if burned with fire and wrapped his hand tenderly around his wrist. "Nay, Lily." He leaned toward her, burying his face in her golden strands. "Lily, I cannot take your maidenhood." He hugged her close.

"Please, Kyle? I need you," she whispered. "No one will know. We are here alone. There is a need that is blossoming inside me. Only you can satisfy it."

"I will know," he whispered. "I will not dishonor you like that. I can give you pleasure in other ways."

Lily had no idea of what he spoke, so she waited to see what he would do next. He positioned her so she was lying on her back on the bed, then rolled onto his side and propped himself on his elbow next to her. "But Kyle, my body is humming for you."

"Hush, sweet one." He took her nipple in his mouth and suckled her until she fell back on the bed, her head on the pillow as she arched her back, showing him what she wanted. His hand moved down to the juncture between her thighs, parting her curls, his fingers finding a spot that made her squeal in response to his touch.

"Hush, and I will take care of you."

His thumb rubbed her tender spot and his fingers found their way inside of her, causing her to spread her legs wider in invitation. "You are so wet for me. Someday you will feel me inside of you. We will be wondrous together, I am sure of it."

"Aye, Kyle." She gripped his arm, unsure of what was happening to her, but trusting him completely. He rubbed and invaded her until she thought she would explode. Her breathing hitched and hitched, as if something needed to happen, but she knew not what. "Kyle, help me. What do I do?"

"Relax and it will happen. Trust my touch." He suckled her nipple again and she gripped her fingers in his hair as a need grew inside her that would not stop, pushing her, tugging her. His teeth scraped across her nipple and she plunged over the edge, her body reacting with such joy she screamed, convulsing around his fingers as he continued his rhythmic strum on her body, until all the tension suddenly left her and she melted in his arms.

"Oh, Kyle. I…"

He smiled, taking her lips in his, a gentle kiss that told her how much he loved her.

"But you…I do not understand. I must do the same for you. Tell me what to do."

He took her hand and placed it on his penis. "Wrap your hand around me, but do not squeeze too hard."

She did as he asked. "Like such?"

He groaned, pulling her closer, cupping her breast with one hand. "Aye, now move your hand up and down. 'Twill not take much. You have teased and tortured me until I am raw with need."

She did what he asked and watched him. He closed his eyes, and she watched his jaw tense, his focus all on one place. How she loved him, how she trusted him, how she wished to do this for him.

"Faster," he whispered.

She did as he asked and he clutched her to him, emitting a deep growl before his seed erupted, and she smiled, knowing she had given him the same pleasure he'd given her. She did not stop until he grabbed her hand, stilling her movement.

"Lily, forgive me." He jumped off the bed, reaching for something to cleanse her hand. "My apologies, I should not…"

Finally finding what he searched for, he returned with a wet cloth and held her hand with such tenderness that the love she felt for him overflowed. "Kyle, do not apologize. I pleased you, did I not?"

He gave her a sheepish look and kissed her, tossing the cloth aside. "Aye, you please me verra much. But I should not have done that. I lose all control around you."

"But I want you to lose control with me. I love you. Is that not the way it should be?" She gazed up at him, hoping he was not about to retreat from her again, as he so often did. She did not understand what drove his moods.

Kyle leaned his forehead against hers, then closed his eyes. "Aye, you have the right of it. You and I together, 'tis the way it should be. Marry me, Lily. Do me the honor of becoming my wife.

Say aye and I'll ask your sire for your hand upon our return."

Lily could not believe what he'd said, but she would not ask him to repeat himself. She threw her arms around his neck and said, "Aye. I'll marry you. I do love you so. Our spirits are enmeshed. We should never be apart. 'Tis the way the heavens and the stars want it. We belong together, forever."

He kissed her deeply, and Lily decided she'd just spent the best day ever with her betrothed. Then he picked up her chemise and handed it to her.

"Kyle, the night is not over. Come to bed with me. I'm tired, and I wish to sleep. You promised to stay with me."

"I know, Lily, and I will stay with you, but not when you're like that."

"Like what?"

"Lily, you need to get your clothes on." He reached for his own tunic and plaid.

"But I do not understand. I prefer to be skin-to-skin with you. 'Tis meant to be. Can you not feel it? Please do not cover yourself." She gave him an appreciative look. "I like your body."

"Aye, I do feel it. 'Tis exactly the problem." He wrapped his plaid around his waist, then returned to the bed.

"Then why do you look at me like that, and why must I cover myself?"

Kyle sighed, staring at the ceiling for a moment.

"Kyle Maule, how can you look at me with such love, touch me so tenderly one moment, and then a few moments later stare at me as if I'm a bug that needs to be squashed?"

Kyle chuckled as he helped her put the night rail back on. "Because, love," he said, wrapping his arms around her. "What we did was wonderful—" he kissed her forehead, "—but it should only happen between two people who are married."

"Nay, 'tis right between us. You have asked me to marry you and I agreed. Why must you reject me?"

"Because we are not yet married, and I dishonored you. Believe me, if your uncle knew of what we did, he'd hang me by my ballocks."

Lily stared off into space, deep in thought. Why, suddenly, it all made perfect sense.

"What is it?" Kyle asked her.

"I was just thinking that now I understand why lads fear being hung by their ballocks."

Kyle couldn't contain his grin, so she laughed and wrapped her arms around his neck.

"I love you, Kyle. But you still have not explained why we must wear our clothes to bed. My aunt and uncle shall not return for another day or two."

"Because. If I feel your skin against me throughout the night, I'll have no self-restraint. You'll not have your maidenhead by the morn, and I'll have to explain to your sire, your brother, and your uncle. Please, for me, just climb into bed and close your eyes. No more talking or teasing me."

Lily kissed his cheek and then bounced on the bed and slid her legs under the covers. "All right, Kyle. In fact, I have the perfect solution."

Kyle climbed in next to her and reached for her to tuck her into his side.

Lily said, "But I have a much better idea. I'll back up to you, just like I do to the fire in the hearth. Then it won't be much of a tease to you."

She rolled until she faced away from him, then tucked herself back up against him for his heat, wiggling her bottom until she was settled nicely against his middle.

Kyle let out the longest groan she'd ever heard from him. She glanced over her shoulder to see his eyes closed and his jaw clenched as if he were gritting his teeth.

She'd never understand lads. She'd tried her best to do him a small favor, and all he could do was sigh and moan.

Would she ever understand him?

⁓

Once Kyle's erection had subsided from the sensation of Lily's soft bottom nestled against him, he'd finally fallen asleep. He'd waited until he heard her rhythmic breathing to close his own eyes.

He'd awakened at dawn to the scent of flowers, only to open his eyes and find Lily staring at him, a smile on her face.

"What is it?"

"Naught. I just like to look at my betrothed. I like your dark hair. It rarely gets mussed up like mine does." She fingered the disheveled locks hanging in front of him. He'd always kept his hair a bit longer than most, allowing it to fall well past his shoulders.

"It seems I've done a fine job fooling you then." He kissed her forehead before he climbed out of bed.

"What do you mean by fooling me?"

Kyle put his breeches on. "Because my hair is always a mess. I rarely comb it."

"Where are you going?" Lily would not tear her gaze from him.

He leaned over to kiss her lips before he moved to the door. "Since the sun is nearly up, I thought I'd get my betrothed some water to refresh herself if she'd be so inclined."

"Aye, my thanks."

"And Lily? Please do not say aught to your aunt and uncle about the betrothal. I'd prefer to speak with your uncle in private first. And when we reach Ramsay land, I'll be speaking to your sire first."

"Whatever you say, Kyle. I had sweet dreams last night."

"I'm pleased." After moving the chest to the side of the door, he picked up the urn on the side table and moved over to the door. "I'll return shortly."

Kyle whistled as he trudged down the passageway. Lily had been so passionate last eve that he'd almost made a huge mistake, but the fear of dishonoring her had been keen enough for him to restrain himself. After he brought the water back to her, he guarded the outside of her door until she was ready for him to escort her to the great hall to break her fast. He'd sent the other guards ahead of them, promising to meet them in the hall.

The day was uneventful. Kyle spent it guarding Lily while she watched the minstrels and the fiddlers who played outside at various times throughout the day. He loved watching the expression of rapture on her face while she enjoyed the entertainers. Her heart was truly delighted by them. He offered to take her back to the fair, but she refused, apparently content to stay near the castle.

The king's steward rushed over to them as soon as they walked into the great hall. Muttering apologies, he requested they take their meal in the great hall that eve.

"The king sends his apologies," he said, "but this is our usual night to open the great hall up to the members of the burgh. He likes to feed the Scots once every sennight. With so many in attendance, the entire staff is needed in the great hall. If this unsettles you, eat early and retire early. The festivities do not become rowdy until later in the eve when the minstrels and the fiddlers arrive after the big meal."

Kyle glanced at Lily to see how she would react to this information. She had enjoyed supping in the private chamber, but they needed to abide by their host's requests.

Lily folded her hands demurely in front of her and gave the steward a wide, warm smile. "We would be most happy to join the festivities in the great hall."

"I think you'll be quite pleased by the fare offered this eve, my lady. Cook is wonderful." The steward beamed and pivoted to return to the kitchens.

Once the steward had left, Kyle said, "I can see through your forced smile. This arrangement does not please you as much as others will believe."

Lily hung her head. "Nay, you are correct. I would rather not be forced to deal with the festivities. But we can eat early and leave, can we not?"

"Of course. I'll do whatever pleases you. I would prefer not to have to guard you in the middle of the chaos that will take place around midnight, I would guess. I am yours to command, my lady." He winked at her and she giggled.

As soon as the hall opened to serve the last meal of the day, Kyle and Lily headed down to the cavernous space with several guards trailing behind them. Two guards were off on other errands Kyle had assigned, but the rest had been ordered to make their way about the periphery of the hall, keeping watch for any unusual guests. Two would be posted just outside the entrance to the hall.

Kyle led Lily inside by the hand, all the while scanning the area for any possible threats. He was not worried by what he saw, for few other guests had arrived at that early hour.

"Kyle, you will sit and eat with me?"

"Lily, much as I would like to, I feel 'tis more important for me to stand guard. I need to keep an eye on what is transpiring in the hall, and if I sit across from you, I will be distracted."

Her face fell, so he searched the room for a possible solution. "Look," he pointed to the center of the room. "There are three lasses about your age sitting together. I would rather you not be alone. They are in the center of the hall, near many of the king's guards. Why not eat with them? I'll take a trencher to eat in the passageway later."

"I'd rather not. You can eat with me."

He squeezed her hand and led her over to the table in the middle. "Nay, I cannot. What happened last night does not change the fact that I have been assigned by our lairds to guard you, and that is what I will do."

"Promise not to leave my side?"

"I promise I will not leave you. I have five Ramsay guards in the hall watching over you and two just outside."

"All right. I'll sit if I must, but I do not wish to stay here for long."

Kyle led her over to the trestle table, his eyes studying every man in the room, trying to become familiar with each of them should they prove a threat. Once they reached the table, he said, "My ladies, this is Lily of Ramsay. Would you mind if she joined your table? Her family has not yet returned from their journey, and she would rather not sup alone."

"Aye, sit with us. I am Fenella, and this is Moira and Kenna. Your hair looks lovely pulled up, but it does not seem verra long."

Lily sat down opposite Fenella, smoothing her skirts. "My aunt likes to fashion my hair in different ways."

Kyle hoped they'd be kind. Lily had tied her hair up, hoping to hide the fact that she'd shorn it off, but lasses rarely missed such details. He moved to the end of the table and stood with his feet apart and his hand on the hilt of his sword.

Moira, the prettiest of the three, leaned toward Lily and said, "Who is he? Do you have your verra own personal guard?"

Lily glanced at him, so he gave her a slight nod to encourage her to say aye to the question. The more people who believed she was carefully guarded, the better.

"Aye. His name is Kyle and he shall guard me until my aunt and uncle return. There are other guards in the area."

Moira giggled. "How lucky you are. Wait until you see all the handsome lads who are coming to the keep to celebrate this eve. They will all come later, but we'd all prefer to eat before they get here."

"Do you come often?" Lily asked.

"Aye," Fenella replied. "We come whenever we can. Kenna is seeking a husband, so we are here to help her."

Moira leaned toward Kenna. "Why do you not ask Lily's guard for a dance this eve? He's quite handsome, though he's a wee bit too big and he leaves his hair too long." She giggled as she lifted her gaze to meet his.

Kyle ignored her, just as he would ignore any lass who tried to tell him his hair was too long.

Lily did *not* ignore her. "You may not have Kyle. He is taken."

"By whom?" Fenella said.

Lily frowned, then said, "He is betrothed to a Ramsay lass, and she is quite pleased with his long hair."

Kyle contained his smirk at Lily's comment. Even more, he wished to stand behind her with his hands on her shoulders, staking his claim for all to see. What pleased him the most was how that one statement seemed to infuse a self-confidence in her, and her statement about his hair was a boon to his self-confidence.

So the wee lass found his hair pleasing. Why did he wish to announce *that* to the entire hall?

"Sounds like *you* are pleased with his long hair," Fenella said. She waggled her eyebrows at Lily, but the moment was interrupted when the serving maids came along with trenchers of stew and bowls of minted peas and onions.

Kyle noticed the strange way Lily was staring at the food. Of course, she could not stomach grains, and would not be able to eat from a trencher. Kyle waved to one of the serving maids, who ran over to see what he needed. "My lady cannot eat from a trencher."

The maid turned to Lily with a scowl, but then said meekly enough, "What can she have?"

"She needs her own bowl, not a trencher, and mayhap some carrots? Do you have any meat besides stew?"

"My, are you not special, Lily." Kenna laughed and rolled her eyes. Kyle did not like the way her two friends looked at Lily either.

Two lads came along and joined them at the table. "And who is the new lassie?" one of them asked.

"This is Lily, Torquil. She needs special food." Fenella tipped her head at Lily.

Just then, the head of the kitchen maids brought some food to

Lily and said, "Here you are, my lady. Forgive me for forgetting your needs." She bowed her head toward Lily and returned to the kitchens.

Torquil had a crooked grin on his face as he stared at Lily, an expression that Kyle was ready to knock off his face with one punch. "Well, we are graced with someone quite special, are we not, Fenella?"

Lily ignored them and began to eat her bowl of peas and carrots. Judging from the speed at which she was shoveling the food in her mouth, Kyle would guess she'd be standing and ready to leave in less than five minutes.

The other lad moved to stand behind Torquil, and he whistled as soon as his gaze settled on Lily. "Will you look at those green eyes, Torquil? Would you not like to see those in the dark?"

Kyle did not know how much more he could take. He reviewed his choices. He could punch them each once, which would probably take care of them, or draw his sword and skewer them. Either choice would make a mess. He decided the king would be upset if such violence should break out so early in the night. So he thought of a different tactic. Anything to get them away without forcing him to raise his fist in the middle of the royal great hall.

The hall was filling up, and more and more people were seating themselves around the tables near them. He did not wish to create a scene. Sweat broke out on his jaw. Finally he said, "Lily, are you ready?"

Torquil stood up. "Nay, she is not. Elliott and I'd like to keep her here." He crossed his arms and faced Kyle with a defiant look on his face. The big lad carried more fat than he did muscle. Even so, Kyle did not wish to act without thinking of the consequences.

Kyle held out his hand. "Lily, let's go."

Lily stood up, the expression on her face telling him how upset she felt. Torquil's friend blocked her path. His arm rubbed her back and he said, "Nay, I think I'll have her, Torquil. We'll allow her guard to watch."

Kyle signaled to his guards, then shifted Lily behind him and lifted Elliot clear into the air. "You'll not touch her again. Ever."

"Put me down. I'll kick your arse. Torquil, get your guards over here to take care of him."

Kyle squeezed his hand around Elliott's neck. "You'll not kick my arse. You'll be a dead man first. Do not touch Lily of Ramsay ever again."

"Lily of Ramsay?" Elliott choked out.

"Aye. What of it? Her aunt and uncle will be here tomorrow, and I do not think you will wish to anger them by doing something foolish." Kyle would use the one card he had that did not involve any bloodshed.

"Who are they? Which Ramsays?" Torquil's face turned pale, and Elliott's smirk slipped fully off his face.

"Mayhap you have heard of them. Logan and his wife Gwyneth?" Torquil began to back away before Kyle had even lowered Elliot to the floor.

"Torquil, get back here and help me," the lad whined. "You promised to stay with me and fight. Are you going to desert a friend in need?"

Kenna whispered, "Is that not the lady who skewers ballocks with her bow?"

Elliott's eyes threatened to pop out of his head at Kenna's revelation. "And they will be here on the morrow?" he managed to choke out.

"Aye," Kyle said, "and you just attempted to molest their favorite niece."

"Nay, not me," Torquil yelled as he started to run. "I'll leave you be."

"Put me down," Elliot said, kicking his legs. "I'll not bother her again."

With that, Kyle flung the lad to the ground. Elliot stood up to run away, but not before he had the last word. "This is not over. I'll make you pay," he snarled.

Kyle led Lily outside, doing his best to calm her. He could hear the whispers flood the hall all around them, but he continued onward, hoping to get her back to her room before the tears started.

"Kyle, do you suppose he could be the one?"

"Which one?"

"Torquil, he was bigger. Or do you think my tormenter could be Elliott?"

"It could be either one of them, Lily, though I'm not sure if Torquil has the stamina to be so bold. Elliott, aye, it could be him."

When they finally reached the top of the stairs, Kyle lowered his hand to the small of her back and guided her toward her chamber. "I'll not let them torment you, Lily." They arrived at her chamber. After checking for intruders, he returned to the door to leave. "You will be all right? There is something I must do, and in view of what just happened below stairs, I think it would be better if I were to protect you from the outside."

"Kyle, you cannot be leaving me, are you?"

Kyle cleared his throat before he swallowed. "My apologies, Lily, but I think it would be best for me not to sleep in here tonight. I'll be just beyond your door."

Lily's face fell so fast, it was as if he'd slapped her.

"Whatever you say." Lily closed the door while he stood in front of it.

He sighed, but he couldn't change his mind. What he had to do was something he had to keep secret from her, and this was the only way he could do it. She'd forgive him later when she understood.

CHAPTER FOURTEEN

To Lily's surprise, her aunt and uncle returned the following day. They strode into the great hall through the front door with their daughters while Lily and Kyle were breaking their fast along with many others. Uncle Logan did not look happy, but Aunt Gwyneth ushered the girls over to their table and requested food for all four of them.

"Uncle, that was a short journey."

"Aye, 'twas too short. And I do not like the implications of it."

"What do you mean?" Kyle asked, rubbing the thumb on his left hand.

Lily stared at Kyle's hand, wondering how his thumb had become so swollen.

"The Buchans ignored the king's request and refused us entry. They claimed it was only because my name is Ramsay, but I see it differently. They have something to hide, and King Alexander will not be pleased with my news."

Gwyneth said, "Please eat something first, Logan. Say good morn to your niece. You can speak with the king later."

Logan kissed Lily on the cheek and sat down. "Aye, just for you, I will."

No longer able to restrain herself from asking the question that had leapt to her tongue, Lily reached over to Kyle's hand. "What did you do to your thumb?"

Gwyneth cast a questioning look at him but said nothing.

"Lily, I explained I had chores to do. One of them gave me trouble."

Logan snorted. "Looks to me like your thumb landed underneath the swing of a hammer." Sorcha and Molly both laughed, but Lily just scowled, wondering why they knew something she did not. What could Kyle have possibly done last night to cause such an injury?

Kyle blushed and hid his thumb under his other arm. "My thumb is of no concern to any of you. 'Tis fine."

At that moment, an unknown lad entered the hall and headed straight for them. Lily frowned at the intruder, wondering why he was coming toward them. Kyle tugged Lily closer to him on the bench.

"Here he comes, Papa," Molly whispered.

Logan spun his head around and said, "There you are, Cormag."

"Aye," the lad said as he sat in the open spot next to Logan. "I thought I would eat with you before I continue on my journey.

"Kyle, do you recall Cormag of Buchan?" Logan asked. "And this is my niece Lily. Cormag has left his clan, so he joined us on our journey back to Edinburgh."

Cormag bowed to Lily. "Aye, I do recall Lily, and I believe I have seen Kyle before."

"Why are you leaving your clan, Buchan?" Kyle asked, a confused expression on his face.

"Because my sister Davina is daft and my sire listens only to her. I'll not stay there. They are headed for trouble, and I do not wish to call the king's army down on my neck. I have several cousins around, and I may join one of their clans. Once I finish breaking my fast, I'll be on my way."

Lily scooted a little closer to Kyle, but did not say a word. Between the two lads last eve and this lad, she was uncomfortable and ready to head home.

They were served bread and cheese, and they all ate in silence until the end of the meal. Cormag finished quickly and got up to leave.

"My lord, I thank you for your hospitality and for allowing me to join you. I'll take my leave. Fine journey to you." Cormag bowed and pivoted toward the door.

"Not sure about that lad, but we must continue."

Logan shrugged and turned to look at Lily. "You look happier today, niece. Is there aught you need to tell me?" Her uncle's gaze narrowed a little as it traveled from her face to Kyle's. If he suspected something, so be it. She had no guilt. She and the man she loved had done naught wrong. They were betrothed and in love.

But she had promised to allow Kyle to speak with her uncle and sire about their betrothal before she announced it to the world. Smiling, she said, "Of course not, Uncle. Kyle and I had a lovely time while you were gone."

"I hope 'twas not too lovely. Must I speak with Kyle?" He glared at Kyle, waiting for his response.

Kyle cleared his throat. "We met two unsavory characters last night, either of them are capable of being Lily's attacker." Lily almost giggled at the way he deflected Uncle Logan's attention like an expert.

"Tell us more." Gwyneth perked up, leaning toward Kyle.

"The king asked us to eat in the great hall last night because he welcomed the burgh's people once a sennight. We decided to eat early to avoid most of the crowd, and Lily sat with three local lasses. 'Twas not long before two lads joined us, each with their sights on Lily."

Logan's face lit up. "How much blood did you spill this time, Maule?"

"I did not shed any, but the two were not at our side for long."

Aunt Gwyneth whispered, "Lily, did you recognize aught about them?"

Lily shook her head. "Nay, I did not, but 'tis still possible, do you not agree?"

Logan said, "Absolutely. What did you notice about them, Maule?"

"Their first stop once inside the hall was Lily's table, and they both had brown hair."

"And their names?"

"Elliott and Torquil. I know naught more, but 'tis enough information to find out more if need be."

"If 'tis all you know, then I'd like to return to the other topic. Do we think the Buchans are planning to attack the Ramsay castle again?" Gwyneth asked. She waved to one of the maids to bring ale to them as they waited for porridge. "Do we need to rush home to head them off, advise your brother?"

"Nay, I do not think they are planning to attack us, but they are for certes planning something." Logan tore off a piece of brown bread that had been set in front of them and motioned to Kyle. "Maule, I'll see you outside for a moment."

Once they left, Lily whispered, "Aunt Gwyneth, what happened on your trip? Uncle did not look at all pleased."

Molly said, "I talked to some of the stable lads while Da argued with the men." Then she giggled. "Lads are such fools. They never suspect that a lass might have a mind of her own. They'll answer my questions, but they'd go mute if Papa tried to ask them the same things."

Gwyneth glanced at her eldest daughter. "Aye, well, the two of you together—" she tipped her head to Sorcha, "—are what unsettles them. I've seen Sorcha tease men to take them off their guard while you find the one who will give you all the information."

"So what did you learn, Molly?" Lily asked.

Molly shook her head. "I was surprised to hear that they all expect the Buchans to go on attack, though they expect way into the Highlands first, which is why Da says he'll warn the Grants. 'Tis all I found out, just that they are ready to battle and be the aggressors. I believe Cormag when he said he does not wish to be part of it."

Sorcha giggled. "She is amusing to watch, Mama. She's adept at using trickery on lads."

"Just be careful, you two. Someday, you'll not have me and your sire there to protect you and you'll get yourselves into trouble."

Logan and Kyle returned by the time all the lasses had finished eating, but Lily had no inkling as to what they'd discussed. She'd hoped Kyle had asked about the betrothal, but she thought there was more to it.

"I'm off to see King Alexander," Logan said, "and when I return, I'll escort you outside for the show. We'll be leaving for home by midday."

Lily sat up and asked, "What show, Uncle? I'd love to watch a show."

"Kyle will explain while we're gone. Gwynie, I'd like you and the girls to meet the king with me."

As soon as they were alone together, Lily stared up at Kyle. "Did you ask my uncle?"

Kyle smiled as he took her hand in his. "Aye, I did. He thought your sire would agree to the marriage once we returned."

"But can we not marry before we leave?" She had no desire to wait. After the things they'd shared, she wanted him with her every night.

"Nay. And you must understand that I need to receive your sire's blessing before we move forward. Do you not wish to have him attend our wedding? I'd like my mother to be there. And what about Lady Brenna, Torrian, and Heather? Do you not want to celebrate with them?"

Lily thought for a moment, then said, "Aye, I would like them to be at our wedding. We'll marry within a sennight upon our return."

"Lily, these things take time. I doubt your parents will be able to prepare for a wedding that quickly. There's no rush, is there? I'll have things I need to tend to with Torrian, as well. I do not see it happening in less than six moons."

"Six moons? Kyle, 'tis a long way from now." Lily's heart was pulled in two directions. Aye, she wanted to celebrate their marriage with their families, but why must they wait?

He chucked her under her chin. "Do not look so defeated. The time shall pass quickly. Come with me. I have a gift for you."

"A gift for me?" Lily hopped off the bench, grabbing the hand Kyle held out for her. She was so excited to hear that Kyle had purchased a gift for her. How she loved opening presents. She'd started making her own packages quite decorative with ribbons instead of using twine and plain packaging, so she was especially fond of brightly wrapped gifts. "Where is my gift, Kyle?" She hurried to keep up with his long strides as he led the way out of the great hall and guided her toward the stables.

He retrieved a wrapped parcel hidden in one of the stalls, nodded to the man in charge, and then guided Lily to an isolated bench. He stood guard while she sat down. "Here. This is for you." He rubbed his swollen thumb.

Lily took the large wrapped gift from him and tugged on the twine to open it. As soon as the wrapping fell away, she gasped. She set the parcel down beside her and jumped up to throw her arms around Kyle's neck. "Kyle, I love it. 'Tis the most beautiful braid I have ever seen. Sunsh…Tilly will love it."

"Lily, 'tis not for your horse, 'tis for you."

She sat down and ran her fingers over the rainbow of colorful ribbons, intertwined and woven into a most beautiful display. It was intricate work, and it must have taken someone hours to make.

He pulled on the piece of wood that held all the ribbons, tugging it away so Lily could see the design he'd made. "See, you can unfold it."

Lily could not believe her eyes. "Did you make this, Kyle? Or did you find it at the fair?"

Logan came along behind them with Gwyneth and the two lasses along with him. He moved over to glance over Lily's shoulder, then whispered to her, "He made it himself. I can vouch for him since I purchased the ribbons before we left for Buchan land. He informed me of his sound plan. Can you not see how he hammered the ribbons to the top of the wood so you can hold it above your head?"

Lily, stunned, unfolded the rest of the braids with Kyle's help, her heart blooming a little more every moment.

"Hold it up," Kyle instructed.

She extended her arm over her head. Oh, how majestic it felt! The ribbons flowed out long behind her, catching on the wind and flying high into the air, much more so than the small one she had made back at her home. The braids fell in waves, and loose ribbons billowed freely at the base of his creation.

"Lily, 'tis quite beautiful," Molly said.

Kyle cleared his throat. "If you'd like, I've arranged for the guards to follow us to a meadow nearby. I sent a couple of them in search of the perfect venue for you last night. You can try it out, see if you can run with it as you did back on Ramsay land."

"Oh, Kyle," she wrapped her arms around his neck and kissed him lightly on the lips. "I love it. 'Tis a wondrous gift." She held it up again, waving it in the breeze to see the colors in the sunlight. "May we go to the meadow today?"

"Lily, 'tis the nicest gift ever, especially if he made it for you," Molly said.

Lily, suddenly recalling her family surrounded her, blushed a deep shade of red at her brazenness. "I will treasure it forever."

Aunt Gwyneth added, "I like it because 'tis a thoughtful gift that speaks to your personality."

"Aye, 'tis perfect time to go now," Logan said. "We would all like to watch you run with the ribbons, Lily. We have a bit of time before we ride back to our keep. But instead of kissing Kyle on the lips, mayhap you might like to kiss the thumb he hit with a hammer trying to make that for you." He gave Kyle a lop-sided grin. "We'll see you in the stables."

With that, Logan headed toward the stables and his family followed. All Lily could do was stare at Kyle. She reached for his hand and kissed his thumb gently. "You did this for me? Truly, Kyle?"

He blushed and said, "I felt terrible for ruining your fun in the meadow. Gwyneth and Logan both told me it was wrong of me, and now I understand. Would you like to go to the meadow to see if this will wave in the wind behind you as the other did?"

She skipped ahead of him, grabbing his hand to tug him toward the stables. "I would love to."

When they arrived at the meadow not long after, Lily tried to leap down immediately, but Kyle held her in front of him for a few moments. "What do you think, love?"

She scanned the area, taking in the autumn colors in the trees and the smell of the surrounding pines. There were a few others walking in the area, enjoying the day. Leaning back against him, she tugged his arm around her waist. "I cannot believe you would do this for me." She squeezed his hand, then kissed his swollen thumb. "Kyle," she pleaded, "I am so excited to try this. There's a lovely breeze today."

"Lily, you must wait until our guards are in place."

Her aunt and uncle were off to the side along with Molly and Gwyneth. Her cousins waved to her, Molly whistling loud enough for all to hear. She knew Molly's game, she was trying to draw as much attention to Lily's show as possible.

Lily enjoyed being held in Kyle's arms and watched as her sire's guards circled the perimeter of the field, unable to believe they would do all this for her. As her uncle rode closer to speak to a couple of guards, she mouthed a thank you to him.

"Do not thank me, thank Kyle. I had naught to do with this. 'Twas his idea to make up for the trouble he caused in the market the other day."

Once they were all set up, Kyle helped Lily down and she took off, running like the wind across the meadow, her laughter tinkling behind her as she twisted and turned, leaping with the long tail of ribbons flying over her head and behind her, a rainbow of colors lighting up the meadow.

Her heart had swelled with the realization that Kyle had to love her for sure to arrange such a thing. She needed no other evidence. She ran and leaped into the air, singing gaily in the fresh air, not caring who watched her.

She was so very much in love.

Kyle watched the joy that poured out of Lily's soul as she ran. Oh, how he loved her. Thank God Logan seemed to think Quade would still be agreeable to the betrothal. The only problem was that Logan had suggested that the marriage take place within a moon, while Kyle preferred the idea of a longer wait. He wanted to make sure he had time to master his new duties before entering into married life. Much as he loved her, Lily was undoubtedly a distraction. Lily clearly didn't want to wait, but he was certain he could convince her.

The sound of her voice carried across the meadow, and more and more people drifted over to listen to Lily, delighting in watching her lithe form as she danced and twirled in the meadow. He could still see her cousins off to the side, cheering her every move. Her humming soon became a song, and the more she sang, the more people clustered near her. Lily was the sweet nectar to a land full of bees.

A voice rang out behind him, one he knew he should recognize.

"Kyle, you are Torrian Ramsay's second still, are you not?"

He glanced over his shoulder. "Aye, I thought you knew that when we discussed this in the royal castle?"

The lad brought his horse up next to Kyle. "I had heard that Quade had made Torrian the new Ramsay chieftain, but I was not sure if you had been promoted along with him."

Once he saw him, he recalled. "Aye, Buchan. Your sire refused a visit from Logan Ramsay. Care to tell me why?"

Cormag sat tall on his horse, brown hair falling over his shoulder. Kyle thought he'd grown a bit since his visit to Ramsay land last year. Though he did not know his age, he guessed him to be under twenty summers.

The lad said, "I left my sire because I do not believe in what he's doing, so I cannot answer for him. I am my own man."

"What is your sire doing that you do not support?"

"My sire speaks only of revenge. He has yet to accept my brother Dugald's death. Sometimes I believe he's become daft over losing his heir, but other times his mind carefully crafts ways to attack his enemies, ways so devious that the verra idea of them make my skin crawl. I try to reason with him, but he does not hear me. As you know, I came to the royal burgh to find another clan to join. I will achieve my goal."

Something about Cormag's tone did not ring true. "But you are his heir now," Kyle said. "Why would you leave and risk losing your rights to your keep? 'Twill be yours when he dies."

"Davina bends him to her will, for one. My sire will do whatever she wishes, but something happened to Davina that she will not admit. She has been addled ever since Dugald and Ranulf died. She startles easily, and oft stares over her shoulder as if a ghost is following her."

"It does not matter if Davina wishes your land. The only way she would have any chance at it would be in the event of your death."

"Mayhap I do not care about our land." He stared straight ahead, watching the show in front of him. "Mayhap I wish for something else."

"And what would that be?" Nay, Kyle did not trust the lad at all.

"I know not, but I am in search of a new life." Cormag sat staring straight ahead, his gaze never leaving Lily.

Kyle decided not to pursue his questioning any further, nor was he at all inclined to invite a Buchan to join the Ramsay clan, if that was the lad's purpose. He needed to keep his focus on Lily. He didn't like what was developing in front of him. More and more people were cramming around the field, anxious to watch the beautiful lass dance and sing as if she had not a care in the world. Oh, how he wished that were true, but it made his nerves prickle to see all those strangers around her.

Kyle understood why Gwyneth had said Lily was a boon to her soul—it was exactly how he felt about her, too. Unfortunately, protecting her was difficult, especially since he was so in love with her. He was watching her so closely that he noticed the instant her happy aura soured to fear.

She swirled around as if lost, screaming his name. Then she dropped her ribbons in the middle of the meadow and started racing as fast as she could, looking so unsettled it plunged him into an instant panic.

Kyle spurred his horse forward, aiming directly for her.

"Kyle, help me!" was all he heard.

CHAPTER FIFTEEN

Lily had sensed the nearness of someone or something with an aura so dark it had frightened her. She knew not what it was, but she was desperate to get as far away as possible from it. Racing back toward the castle, she scanned the crowd for any sign of Kyle, her uncle and aunt and her cousins. Why had she not paid closer attention to where she was going?

She screamed in the hope the sound of her voice would reach Kyle. Breathing a sigh of relief, she noticed three horses heading straight toward her. How far down the meadow had she traveled? Two of the horses were headed straight for her, and the one approached from the side. The horses in front of her would reach her first.

Why two? Kyle was on one, she could sense it, but who was on the other? Uncle Logan? As soon as they came close enough, she recognized Kyle.

"Lily, what is it?" Kyle had come for her as fast as he could. She could sense the tension in his body, see him panting from exertion. Thank goodness he'd heard her.

"Help me, Kyle. Please!" She held her arms out to him as she raced forward. Just as he slowed his horse to reach for her, another horse crossed in front of him, its rider reaching down to grab her. She jerked out of the way at the last moment because she could not tell who reached for her.

Overwhelmed with fear, she ran screaming from the unknown rider. The two horses danced around her, causing her to lose all sense of direction, and she stretched her arms upward as she searched for her love.

"Kyle! Kyle!"

"Lily! Hold still and I'll get you."

The unknown horseman came toward her again, and she shrieked, wrapping her arms around herself and closing her eyes. She heard a sword being unsheathed just as Kyle shouted, "Get back, Buchan. You'll not touch her."

"I was only trying to assist you."

A whistle echoed through the air, followed by a stampede of horses, the pounding of their hooves vibrating the ground underneath her feet. She covered her head and did her best to stay away from the two forces parrying near her as the rest of the Ramsay guards headed in their direction.

She heard the whinny of a horse next to her and opened her eyes just in time to see the horse up on its hind legs. Afraid she was about to be trampled, she ran in the opposite direction, but there were too many horses around, and she knew not what to do. Spinning in a circle, a voice broke through the chaos.

Kyle, her savior. "Lily, hold still. Open your eyes, Lily. Can you hear me?"

She froze in the middle of the chaos, doing as Kyle asked, praying he would rescue her from this madness. An arm reached down for her and tossed her into the air as if she were no more than a butterfly—Kyle's, she knew it—before catching her and settling her down on the saddle in front of him. She glanced over her shoulder to smile at him, though she wished to cling to him and never let go.

"Hang on, love. I've got you."

Lily turned on her side and tucked herself up against Kyle's powerful chest, closing her eyes against all the dust flying through the air. Uncle Logan appeared next to them, shouting, "She hale?"

Kyle glanced down at her, and she squeezed his hand, nodding.

"To the stables," Logan bellowed, riding off after Gwyneth and his daughters.

Lily was petrified, unable to move. She had no idea where the evil aura had come from, but *he* was here, she was sure of it. The man who had tried to kidnap her on two occasions was in the crowd somewhere. She buried her face in Kyle's chest, bouncing against him, wanting so desperately for him to take her away from here—for him to take her home.

As soon as they reached the stables, Logan led their guards off to the side, leaving Gwyneth and the girls with Lily and Kyle.

"Lily, are you all right?" Gwyneth asked.

She pulled her tear-stained face away from Kyle long enough to nod to her aunt, though she could not bear to untwine her arms from his waist. When he stopped his horse, he ran his hand down her back and settled his chin on top of her head, holding her close the way she loved most.

Molly shouted, "Lily, who were those others around you?"

Sorcha added, "I've never seen such a melee on horseback. I was so afraid you'd be trampled. That man, the one whose horse reared, I could not tell who he was. I thought he'd hurt you for sure."

"What happened, Lily?" Logan asked when he returned to them.

"*He* was there."

"Who was there?"

She pushed away from the comfort of Kyle's chest long enough to say, "The lad who tried to kidnap me."

"Which one was he? There was no one in the meadow besides you. Did he yell at you from one of the sides?"

She shook her head, burying herself in Kyle's chest again.

"Lily?" Kyle whispered. "Help us find him, sweeting."

She looked at each of them in turn. "You'll not believe me."

Uncle Logan said, "Lily, you must tell us what you know. We cannot help if you do not tell us."

She sniffled and closed her eyes, tears flooding her cheeks. "I never saw him, but I could feel him. He was there. He has an evil presence." She opened her eyes to see if her uncle believed her, but she could tell he did not. "Uncle Logan, I knew you would not believe me."

Logan pulled his horse closer. "Lily, 'tis not that I do not believe you, but that I do not understand."

But how could she explain a feeling? There had been no tangible evidence of the man's presence, and yet she *knew* it had been him. Lily decided it was too difficult to put into words. "Please take me home. I hate it here. I want to see Papa again."

It hadn't taken long for them to gather their belongings and leave. Molly, bless her soul, had even ridden back to the meadow to retrieve Lily's ribbons with her sire trailing her.

They settled in a clearing that night. The guards were busy roasting rabbits, and Lily sat on a log next to Kyle. She reached for his hand and asked, "Who was the man on the other horse? I know you told me, but I could not focus on aught this morn."

Logan and Gwyneth were sitting on a log across from them, and Molly and Sorcha had just returned from the woods with a sack full of nuts and berries they were busy sorting.

"Nay, you could not focus on me at all," Kyle said with a small smile. "You must have been exhausted from what happened in the meadow. I've not seen you sleep that hard. You slept in front of me for the entire journey."

"You kept me up the other night or do you not recall?" she whispered. "I needed to catch up."

Molly gave her a quick glance, making Lily wonder as if she'd heard them, but at least Aunt Gwyneth and Uncle Logan seemed too distracted by their own conversation to pay any mind to them.

Through a mouthful of berries, Sorcha asked, "Aye, who was the daft man who tried to lift Lily onto his horse?"

"Cormag Buchan," Kyle replied. "The lad who says he wants to join a different clan. I'm not sure I trust him, but who could blame him for wanting to leave the Buchans?"

"But why was he chasing Lily?" Molly asked.

"He claimed he was trying to help. We were talking on one side of the meadow when Lily started to run. I really do not think he had any ill intention."

"I do not like him," Lily said.

"Well, I can't say I approve of what he did, but it tends to get people excited when a lass starts screaming like that in the middle of a bunch of horses. We had no idea what had happened to you."

Sorcha giggled as she tossed a berry to Lily. "I thought 'twas a bee the way you turned daft and dropped your ribbons."

"My thanks for retrieving them, Molly. I could not bear to lose them." She cast a sheepish glance at Kyle, but he did not respond.

Truth was, she could not explain what had come over her in that meadow. She just had *known* something was wrong. It was as if a dark curtain had fallen over her happiness in an instant.

She stood up, whispering to Kyle, "I must relieve myself."

"I'll go with you."

"Nay, can I not go by myself? 'Tis verra embarrassing to have you nearby listening to me." She gave his side a light poke.

Molly jumped up. "I have to go, too. We can go together. Will that suit you, Kyle?"

Kyle frowned, but Lily tugged on his hand, "Please? If we are not back in a moment or two, you can follow us."

"I'll follow you whether you like it or not, but if Molly is with you, I'll stay back a bit more," he said with a growl.

Uncle Logan's gruff laughter filled the clearing. That time he *had* been listening.

Molly took Lily's hand and led her to a spot off behind a group of bushes. "If we continue to talk, Kyle will not be able to hear aught else."

Lily chuckled. "What a great idea. What kind of berries did you find in the woods?"

Their conversation continued until she was finished. As soon as Lily had herself together, she stood and stretched. Molly was nearby, but she heard rustling in the bushes in the opposite direction.

"Kyle?"

He didn't answer.

"Kyle?"

Molly joined her, and the two huddled together in the bushes. "Kyle, where in hell did you go?"

They heard more rustling, so Molly grabbed her hand and said, "Come, we must get back. He must be playing a trick on us."

Lily took her hand and followed her. But as soon as they turned back toward camp, two men appeared out of the bushes and lunged toward them—dirty, frightening strangers. Lily dropped Molly's hand in a fit of terror and shrieked as she fled in the opposite direction.

She ran right into another man's arms, and he whispered, "Do not worry, I told you I love you. I'll love you forever."

Lily stared into the man's face in shock. She opened her mouth to scream, but blinding pain shot through her head, and her world went black.

CHAPTER SIXTEEN

Kyle grabbed his head as soon as he awakened, and the first thing he discovered was sticky, wet blood all over his head and his face.

Lily.

He pushed himself to a sitting position. "Kyle," a familiar voice said. Only then did he realize that Gwyneth was beside him. "Kyle," she repeated, "Logan has taken several guards and gone after her. I'm sure they'll find her. Now tell me what you remember."

He rubbed his face, clearing the blood away as best he could, wiping much of it on his sleeve as he cursed himself for having failed Lily yet again. "I was about to go after Lily and Molly when I turned my head to see two men bearing down on me. I tried to pull my sword in time, but they struck me in the head before my hand could reach the hilt. Are they both gone?"

"Lily is gone, but we found Molly a ways from here. She was knocked out like you were, and does not remember aught that happened. She's frightened and worried for her cousin, but she'll be fine. The evidence points to four men on horseback. They must have taken care of you before they went after Lily and Molly."

"Where the hell were our guards? What were they doing?"

"Some were hunting, and two were knocked out, hit in the head as you were."

Kyle stood up, weaving a bit, but managed to right himself and head toward his horse. "I must go after them. Logan needs my help."

Sorcha stepped in front of him and held up fingers. "How many do you see?"

"Three, and I also see a lass I'll be forced to knock out of the way if she does not move."

"Kyle," Gwyneth said. "You're not thinking straight. She only has two fingers up. You could do more harm than good chasing after them when you're likely to fall off your horse."

"I do not care. 'Tis my fault. I allowed the lasses to talk me into keeping a wider distance for their foolish privacy. Now look what's happened. I must go after Lily. How many on horseback?" He made it to his horse and mounted, though it took him a while to straighten up. Hellfire, it must have been a huge rock that hit him.

Gwyneth followed him. "I told Logan you'd be behind him. He kept Molly with him in case she remembers something that will assist them in their investigation. Take two more guards with you. We've also sent a messenger home requesting more guards. We think there are four horses." Gwyneth whistled and two more men approached them through the trees. "Mount up," she ordered them. "You're going with him. They headed north."

But Kyle could not wait. He flicked the reins of his horse, heading north. The guards would have to catch up to him. His head felt like ten lads were inside his head pounding tiny hammers in an attempt to get out, but he would not let that stop him.

He had to find his Lily. He could not lose her.

He would be lost without his love.

When Lily finally awakened, she stared at her surroundings in bafflement. She was on a soft bed, buried under a pile of furs, in a cottage that was well cared for and clean.

Where in hell had he taken her?

She sat up, intent on searching the small room for any clues, only to fall back down on the bed. Her head had started pounding furiously the moment she moved. Now she remembered. She'd been hit in the back of the head.

Where was Molly?

Where was Kyle?

What had he done to them?

A face appeared in the doorway of the small chamber. "Good, you are awake. How is your head? I am sorry, but I had to knock you out so you would not yell. Please forgive me."

Cormag Buchan moved toward her, and she held her hand up to

stop him. "Keep away from me, Cormag. I want naught to do with you." She moved her legs to the side of the bed, planning to get down, but he was at her side in a moment.

"But I love you, Lily. I fell in love with you when we came to your land. I've never seen a lass as kind and beautiful as you are. But you ignored me the entire time we were there. I had to get you for myself. Do not be afraid of me. You will fall in love with me in time. I am sure of it."

Lily froze. Now she recognized his voice. "You? 'Twas you who followed me? Even back on Ramsay land?" Her heartbeat sped up as she realized the implications of what he was saying.

He'd been planning this for a long, long time.

Was he telling the truth? Had she ignored him? She thought back to the time he'd been at Ramsay land, when Davina had come with her sire. There was a time when she'd been in the hall during the festivities, and she'd caught Cormag staring at her. He had never spoken to her, so she understood why she'd never recognized his voice, but had it started back then?

He'd been there in the stable when she'd been caring for Sunshine, and when she'd been talking to her mother once. Then she'd noticed him by the hearth staring at her. Every time she saw him, he'd turned away.

Why hadn't she thought of him before? Because he wasn't the first lad to stare at her.

"Where are Kyle and Molly?"

"I do not want Molly. Forgive me, but I needed to knock out Kyle and Molly and two of your guards. My men, unfortunately for you, enjoy striking people daft. 'Tis one of their specialties. I hired them for that reason. They'll be fine when they awaken. If you'd just agreed to come with me when I approached you near your keep, none of this would have happened. I would not have been forced to steal you away and hurt the others. Why did you not wish to come with me?"

"Cormag, I do not want you. I love another. Please set me free, and I'll not tell anyone what you've done." Climbing down from the bed, she bent over to place her boots on her feet, sending a shooting pain through her head. "Ahhh...I do not care if it hurts. I must leave now."

He stood in front of her and took both of her hands in his. "I'm sorry, Lily. But you're not going anywhere. You're going to be my wife, and we'll live here happily for the rest of our lives, many bairns surrounding us. I've taken great care to fill this cottage with everything you could possibly want: soft linens, warm furs, a big hearth for winter, and many tapestries on the wall. Look at all the wood I have chopped to keep you warm." He pointed to a chest that hulked to one side of the bed. "I even had beautiful gowns and night rails made for you. You'll learn. We'll be happy forever."

Lily's gaze narrowed at him, wondering what had happened to addle him so. "I'll not be marrying you, Cormag Buchan. I belong to Kyle Maule, and I'm leaving now." She attempted to shove him aside, but he was too big for her tiny frame.

Instead, he shoved her back on the bed and climbed on top of her, holding himself up on his elbows as he gazed into her eyes. "You did not hear me. I love you, and you'll learn to love me in return. Kyle made a big mistake, and now you'll be mine."

Lily did her best not to cry.

"My love, why did you cut your hair? 'Twas the most beautiful hair of all. I was verra upset when I noticed you'd shorn your locks."

"Then let me go. I like my hair short."

"Nay, your hair will grow back. I can wait." He leaned down and placed a chaste kiss on her lips. "You're mine forever."

Kyle didn't have to go far before he came upon Logan and Molly. "Is Molly all right?"

Logan had Molly on his horse. "I sent my guards ahead. Molly's not feeling well, and her memories haven't returned to her. I'm going to leave her with Gwyneth, but ride on, and I'll catch up with you."

Kyle urged his horse on, but Molly yelled out to him at the last instant. "Kyle, I do recall something."

He stopped and turned to look at her. "What is it?"

"Cormag. I'm sure it was Cormag Buchan's voice I heard just before I was hit in the head."

Kyle would kill the bastard.

Lily had thought hard before deciding on her best course of

action. She would pretend to accept him. It would be far easier to deal with Cormag if he trusted her. And indeed, she had convinced him to give her some space by claiming she needed to sleep because of her headache. He'd left her alone in the chamber and closed the door behind him.

She pinched her cheeks and straightened her gown before she walked over to the door, only to find it locked from the outside.

"Cormag, I'm hungry. May I come out to find something to eat?" She felt like spewing all over her boots, but she used her sweetest voice and plastered her best smile on her face. With any luck, she would be able to hold it in until she could aim her vomit on his boots instead of her own.

She heard the bolt being lifted and folded her hands in front of her in an effort to look more innocent. As soon as she saw his face peeking around the door, she said, "Good eve to you, Cormag. May I please be allowed out to eat something?"

Cormag stood back, watching her warily as he opened the door wider. "Will you promise not to run?"

"Aye, I promise. 'Struth is I'm much too tired to run tonight. This has been an exhausting journey for me, and I wish to sleep well into the morn. But I must put an end to the rumbling in my belly first."

Cormag took a step back to allow her to exit the chamber. She moved into the main chamber. There was a large hearth at one end with two chairs and a small table in front of it. There were many cooking utensils about, including several knives. There were dried flowers in vases and embroidered cushions on the chairs.

Striding toward one of the chairs in front of the hearth, she made a point of taking in everything around her. "My, but this is lovely, Cormag. Whose cottage is this?" She sat in the chair and folded her hands in her lap.

Still frowning, he moved to the pot hanging on the hearth to dish a bowl of stew for her, then set it on the table next to her. "I've arranged everything, Lily. I've been fixing this ever since I left the Ramsay land. I knew you loved me then, as I love you. Though 'twas a challenge to get away from my sire to make it all fitting for you. Do you like it?"

"You did a fine job. 'Tis most comfortable here. May I eat now?"

Cormag nodded as he filled a second bowl for himself. "Aye. 'Tis boar stew. I cooked it special for you. There are no grains in it as I know you cannot eat them. I was verra careful."

Lily took a bite and fought to keep from spewing the ill-tasting concoction across the room. Forcing herself to swallow, she reminded herself that she would need her strength to escape this daft man.

She ate every bit of the foul stew, then stood, stretching her arms above her head and yawning. "May I return to bed, please? I am verra tired. I need my rest. My mama always told me I need to sleep more than most."

Cormag fussed over her, taking her bowl to the basin before helping her to the next chamber as if she were an invalid. "Lily, I'll get you the nice night rail. You may wear it tonight." He ran to the chest and pulled out the skimpy garment, setting it on the bed.

So far everything had gone according to Lily's plan. There was only one problem—she knew she'd have to do the unthinkable.

Cormag nodded to her, his cheeks going pink, and then left the room and bolted the door behind him. Aye, there was only one way she could free herself from him. At least it was dark already. She donned the night rail, but left her gown close by so she could put it over the thin shift later. She found a small sack and hid it under the bed, then climbed into bed, getting her night rail situated under the furs.

Dear Lord, please help me get through this.

After waiting a few moments, she sighed for strength and then yelled out to her captor, "Cormag, 'tis cold in here. Will you not warm me?"

She could hear him fumbling with the wooden bolt on the other side of the door. When he stepped inside, he stared at Lily with wide eyes. "You would like me to keep you warm?"

"Aye, but my head does hurt from the blow you delivered earlier, so I hope you would not take advantage of a lass in pain." She fluttered her eyelashes at him, then cast her gaze down at her hands folded in her lap.

Cormag came in, tripping over his own feet before he yanked his boots off and tossed them into one of the corners. "Lily, my sweet Lily. I'll do whatever you ask. I just want to hold you in my arms."

She settled back against the pillow. "You know I'm shy, Cormag. Please put the tallow out and come warm me." She closed her eyes, waiting and praying he would do as she asked.

When he climbed in next to her, she did her best not to gag. The lad needed a bath. She closed her eyes and thought of Kyle, the love of her life, how his scent was so pleasing to her. How she hoped he was out there searching for her. She turned away from Cormag as he snuggled up to her, but he honored one of her requests—he did not touch her inappropriately. This was necessary, she reminded herself. He had to think he could trust her. Though it sickened her to touch him, she even patted the hand he wrapped about her middle.

Much later, after several spells of Cormag coughing and reaching for her, he finally fell asleep. His light snores were quite rhythmic. Each time he moved in his sleep, she managed to sneak a little further away from him. He let out a loud snore and rolled onto his back, so she hopped out of bed. Standing still at the side, she held her breath and waited.

After a few minutes passed without him moving, she donned the gown over the night rail, grabbed her boots and the sack under the bed and tiptoed into the main chamber, thankful he hadn't closed the door to the bed chamber. Closing it behind her, she barred the door. She put on her boots and mantle, grabbed two knives from the table along with a hunk of cooked meat and two oatcakes, and sneaked out the front door.

Once outside, Lily raced as fast as her wee legs would go, running between trees and bushes, hoping she could get far, far away before he missed her. Unfortunately, she had no idea which direction to go. She could only follow her gut, praying all the while Kyle would find her before Cormag awakened and followed her.

CHAPTER SEVENTEEN

Kyle eventually caught up with the other guards, who were standing on one side of a small creek. Hellfire, he hoped they hadn't found anything bad.

He took a deep breath and moved up beside them. "What's wrong?"

The guard looked up at Kyle. "We lost their trail in the creek."

"They must have crossed it."

"We cannot pick the trail up on the other side. It appears he moved through the stream for a while to lose us. It worked."

"There are only two directions to go, upstream or down. You take your guards and head upstream, and I'll head that way."

The guards nodded in agreement, but Kyle did not wait for them to say anything. He was already down the stream. He could not afford to wait and converse.

Lily ran and ran until she could run no more. She wished she'd grabbed a water skin, but she hadn't thought of it. A fine warrior she would make. Leaning against a tree, she took stock of her surroundings. It was still the middle of the night, but a full moon helped light the way for her. Once her breathing slowed, she stopped to listen, certain she'd heard something unusual.

Oh, how she wished this was not happening to her. She did not want to be alone in the dark, in a strange land, fighting for survival. Molly or Sorcha would know what to do, but she had no skills out here in the wild. Worried it might be a snake or a threatening animal, she held her breath to see if the sound continued. It came again, a distant whining, a weak cry for help.

Her lack of accomplishments had come back to haunt her. She

should have paid more attention to her mama's teachings. All she could do was sing and twirl and make people smile. If someone or something was out here and in pain, she could do naught to help. She had no skills. She wished to walk away, but Lily could not ignore the pained cries.

She crept in the direction of the sound, then stared wide-eyed as she found the source of the cries. A wolf lay pinned beneath a downed tree, unable to move. Lily moved closer to assess the poor animal's situation. The tree appeared to have been hit by lightning, which meant it had happened a while ago since there had not been any storms in the last day or so.

Moving closer to the wolf, she sat far enough away to be out of its reach.

"Oh, what a beauty you are, Mr. Wolf. You have the prettiest eyes I've ever seen." She reached out to pet him, but he growled at her, so she jerked her hand back.

"Hmmm. My guess is you've been there a while, so you must be quite hungry. I do not wish to be your next meal." She walked around the tree to see if she thought she could move it, finding a long broken branch along the way. "I believe I can set you free, but how do I know you will not attack me once you're free?"

She pondered this dilemma for a moment, then returned to her sack and pulled out the large hunk of cooked meat she'd grabbed off the table from Cormag. She stared at it a good while, then said, "Mr. Wolf, I do believe you need this more than I do."

Carefully, she held it out to the wolf and he snapped it out of her hand, chewing on it as if he had not eaten in days. Lily believed in the innate goodness in animals, and she had to hope he wouldn't go after her if he had a full belly, or at least partly full. If she saved him, he would not kill her. Or would he? Eyeing him carefully, she decided she would have to trust him, so she allowed him time to eat his small meal before she did what she needed to do. As soon as he finished, she said, "I think 'tis time to try to free you, Mr. Wolf. Please promise me you will not attack me if I set you free."

The wolf never took his gaze off Lily, which unsettled her a bit, but she was not the type of person who could leave and let one of God's beautiful creatures die. She knew what she had to do. Humming to hide her fear, she moved over to the tree and tried to lift it enough for the wolf to pull himself out, but she couldn't make it budge.

"Hmmm…it appears I need Kyle's muscular arms, yet I have none." Locating the large branch she'd grabbed, she moved closer to see if she could somehow use it to leverage the wolf out of his trap. Not realizing it, she'd moved close enough to the wolf for him to lean toward her.

She jerked back in fear, but then giggled.

The wolf licked her.

"I hope I do not taste verra good to you, but you are one of God's sweet creatures, so I will do what I can to free you." Setting to her task, she moved the branch under the tree to act as a lever, then pushed down on it as hard as she could.

Nothing happened at first, but just before she was to give up, the tree moved a bit, just enough for the wolf to pull himself free.

Lily let go of the branch and the tree fell back in place. She jumped in the air, clapping her hands as she watched the wolf pace the small area around the tree, stumbling, falling, and righting himself several times. Once his movements improved, he headed off, probably to find his pack, but then he stopped and turned to look at her, his gaze quite intent. Lily sat down on the felled tree, waiting to see what the animal would do. If he wished to attack her, she knew she'd be helpless.

He was a huge beast, muscular and taller than any of the wolves she'd seen from a distance. He crept toward her and stopped about a foot's length away, close enough for her to see his haunting blue eyes.

"I think you need a name, Mr. Wolf. Hmmm. Allow me to consider this for a moment." Her finger tapped her lip as she stared into the starlit sky. "Moonbeam. 'Tis what I'll call you. Moonbeam, are you all right? I'm sure your pack is not far away." She giggled. "Do tell them not to attack me, if you please."

Moonbeam didn't move; he just stared at her and took in her scent. "For certes, you can smell that I am no threat to you, Moonbeam. Have you come to thank me for setting you free?" Not knowing what else to do, she held her arms out to him and said, "You wish to express your appreciation, do you not? Aye, then come and I'll give you a hug in return. A hug will make your day much better."

The wolf hesitated, but then walked into her arms and licked her cheek. She giggled and wrapped her arms around him, but then she remembered her purpose.

"I admit 'twas lovely meeting you, Moonbeam, but it's time for me to move on. I must find the man of my dreams, Kyle Maule. If you wish to walk with me, you're welcome to."

To her surprise and delight, Moonbeam followed right behind her—limping along—when she set off. At one point near dawn, her throat was so dry due to lack of water that she was forced to stop to hack and cough. Moonbeam moved ahead of her, so Lily waved goodbye to him since she was unable to speak. Surprisingly, he stopped a distance away and turned around to stare at her, as if he were beseeching her to follow.

Lily moved behind him, and Moonbeam led her over to a stream with a small waterfall, enough for Lily to place her hands underneath the cool fluid and pour it over her face before she drank from it. Moonbeam drank his fill beside her before they continued.

But not before Lily gave him another hug for leading her to the water. "There, Moonbeam. I helped you and you have helped me. Many thanks to you. If you wish to find your pack, I'll understand."

She swore Moonbeam snorted.

Kyle moved downstream and found what he'd hoped to find—the tracks of three horses. He followed them for a short distance only to become totally confused. The tracks split, one horse had moved in a completely different direction than the other two. The tracks were different, and he stared at them for a moment.

"Nay," Kyle whispered to himself, the importance of the difference finally dawning on him. The single set of tracks was deeper than the other two. "This set is deeper because there were two on the horse—Cormag and Lily. 'Tis where I'm headed."

Kyle flicked the reins and shot off after the direction of the one horse. Cormag was alone with his beloved. His mind filled with horrible thoughts. The lad undoubtedly had a sword, but would he truly be able to fight off boar or wolves, should it come to that? And even if they reached their destination safely, Lily would be at the lad's mercy...

Kyle rode until darkness descended and more. He'd thought of every possible scenario and none of them were good. He adored his Lily, but she was not a fighter, and that worried him more than he would like. He thought of how Heather had stabbed her attacker in the back, slowing him down enough for Torrian to finish him off, of how Heather, Molly, and Sorcha were all adept enough with a bow and arrow to kill. Lily was too sweet to do such a thing. He doubted she could kill anyone outright.

Then a comforting thought occurred to him. Lily was a fighter, just not with a sword or a bow and arrow. Hadn't she lost her mother as a wee bairn and fought a horrid disease?

Aye, the woman he loved would fight, but in her own way. He saw something out of the corner of his eye, and a voice in his head told him to go back. A cottage sat hidden in a copse of trees. He dismounted his horse and threw the reins over a tree branch. After pausing for a moment to consider the situation, he drew his sword and advanced on the cottage. There was one thing that punched a fist into his gut.

The hut was too silent.

He crept around the outside of the cottage, noticing there was no fire in the hearth at present. A sigh released from him as he peered into the window.

The cottage appeared to be empty. He sheathed his sword and stepped inside to see if he could detect any clues. He was surprised at what he discovered in the main chamber. The hut was clean and orderly. Plenty of wood sat in a pile by the hearth, and there was fresh bread and fruit on the counter. He headed into the second chamber, which was equally empty, although it was once again clear someone had been here. On his way out, he noticed something amidst the rushes on the floor. He bent over to retrieve it, and the first thing he did was bring it up to his nose.

It was a ribbon, and it smelled just like his Lily did.

She'd been here for certain.

Lily and Moonbeam traveled for quite a while. She'd expected to hear sounds of Cormag following her, but thus far, she'd evaded him. But one glance at the sky was all she needed to tell her that their troubles were far from over.

"Moonbeam, look at those dark clouds rolling in. We're about to be drenched. Can we not find a spot to hide until the storm blows over?" Dawn was almost upon them, but the storm clouds would block out the sun. She knew what was coming, and as much as she loved nature, she had no desire to run through the forest during a thunderstorm. Where would they go? Frantically searching for a cave or an old deserted cottage, she picked up her pace until she was tearing through the trees.

A sudden streak of lightning lit the sky, causing Lily to scream and jump. How she wished for her sire to protect her. She raced blindly until a short howl stopped her in her tracks. Moonbeam had sat down in front of her, and was waiting to lead her to safety—or so she hoped. She followed Moonbeam, who led her through a maze that became darker and more overgrown with each step. Flashes of light followed by crashes of thunder rent the air, causing Lily to run with her arms wrapped around herself tight, almost running blindly. How she hoped Moonbeam would help her. Would she ever find her way out?

Her mantle and hood were so wet that she began to shiver helplessly as Moonbeam led her up a small hill. It was slippery because of the wet moss and stones, but Lily clung to rocks along the side of the small ravine until she reached the top. Moonbeam was waiting for her there, and he nuzzled her hand when she joined him. She peered straight ahead and found herself staring at the mouth of a cave, hidden from the forest by a large rock.

Once inside, a flurry of lightning streaks lit up the sky as if warning her of what was to come. Moonbeam shook his fur three times to rid himself of the drenching raindrops. Lily tossed the sack aside, removing her mantle only to find her gown partially wet as well. She stripped that off, leaving her in the night rail Cormag had given her. While she wished to tear it to shreds, she knew it was her only protection against the elements at the moment. Glad to be inside the cave, it was still cold and hard stone, naught to give her any heat.

Hanging her wet mantle on a high stone in the wall, she then moved to take care of her gown. She folded it so the driest part was on the top, then she lay on the stone, resting her head on the damp gown. Much as she tried, she could not quell the quiet sobs and shivers racking her body. Moonbeam lay down opposite her, his nose resting on her hand. When her crying slowed, Moonbeam gave her a small whine and nuzzled her hand before moving to the back of the cave, stopping to see if she would follow him. When she didn't move, he nudged her a bit harder, so she finally got up to see what he wished her to do.

He led her toward the back of the cave, down through a dark maze that she would never have followed on her own, but Moonbeam's quiet breathing soothed her enough for her to take the chance. The cave turned brighter and she found herself in a larger cavern with a bit of light streaming in from a small opening at the top. The wolf moved to the center of the cave and sat down, waiting for Lily to come abreast of him.

"Moonbeam, I do not understand what you are trying to tell me. Aye, 'tis a bit warmer back here, but I'm still shivering." Moonbeam held fast in his position, his tongue lolling as if waiting for her. He gave a short howl, but she couldn't guess what he was trying to tell her. She waited for her eyes to adjust to the wee bit of light in the cavern, and her eyes widened. Water? Was she looking at a small pool? Moving up, she knelt down next to her friend, leaning over to feel the coolness of the water.

Only it wasn't cold; it was quite warm. As her hand sunk into the heat of the spring, she let out a small moan of joy. Removing her hand, she leaned over Moonbeam and wrapped him in her arms. "My thanks, Moonbeam. 'Tis exactly what I need."

She stripped off her night rail and set it down on a nearby rock. Moonbeam led her around to the back of the pool, where a small ledge jutted out over the water. It was the ideal spot to sit and dip her feet into the pool. She lowered both feet into the water and wallowed in the warmth of it. Leaning forward, she lapped the water up over her shoulders to warm herself, enjoying every moment. The wolf moved over to the edge and stuck his face in to lap up a drink, then finished by licking Lily's arm until she giggled and planted a kiss on top of his head.

"Oh, Moonbeam, I do love you so. I hope you'll stay with me forever."

He lowered himself to the stone floor, resting his head next to Lily's arm.

After a glorious bath, Lily climbed out, walking around until her skin dried off because she wished to keep her night rail dry. Once she was dressed, she returned to the mouth of the cave. The storm continued to rage in all its glory beyond their shelter.

How would Kyle ever find her in this mess? She couldn't imagine searching for someone in this storm. Uncle Logan was one of the best trackers in the land, but this storm would wash all her tracks away. How would they find her?

She hoped it also meant that Cormag would end his pursuit until the storm calmed down. If Cormag managed to find her in the cave, she hoped Moonbeam would protect her. She moved to the back of the cave again, totally exhausted, and fell asleep with only her night rail on, curled up on a section of her gown that was now dry. Moonbeam stood guard at the mouth of the cave.

Much later, Lily found herself back in that old place, the one she so feared.

In the trees.

She was tethered to the tree all over again—a helpless, lost, and lonely child. Awakening with a cry, she wrapped her arms around herself. It was an awful dream, but she knew why it had plagued her again.

She was as lost and alone now as she had been then. Her worst nightmare had come to pass.

But nay, she was *not* alone. Moonbeam had nuzzled against her to give her his heat, and she was surprised at the comfort of his warmth. Her fingers ran through his soft fur and he lifted his head to lick her, rolling onto his back. The sound of heavy rain still echoed through the chamber, but the thunderstorm had stopped.

The sun had come up, so she made her way to the opening to look outside, but there was no sign of anyone coming to her rescue. She stood at the cave entrance and dissolved into sobs.

"Kyle, Kyle, save me, please!" she shouted.

She cried and cried until she had no more tears.

Moonbeam howled at her feet.

CHAPTER EIGHTEEN

Kyle's confidence waned. Where in hell could Lily possibly be? He'd searched the area completely, following the tracks of one horse he'd picked up leaving the cottage, but had come up empty, losing the tracks at the stream again. This horse had been different, suggesting only one rider instead of two.

If so, and the horse carried Cormag, then where the hell was Lily? He reviewed everything he'd been taught by Quade and Logan, Seamus and Mungo, all of his teachers he'd listened to over the years about tracking.

On a fluke, he decided to try a different route. His excitement grew when he caught fresh tracks heading in a direction he hadn't anticipated. He spurred his horse ahead, crashing through the bushes to catch up with the lone horseman. Quite sure it was Cormag, he rested his hand on the hilt of his sword to make sure it was easily accessible. If he had to kill the bastard to find out where Lily was, he would do so without hesitation.

Time passed, and a thunderstorm had moved into the area, lighting up the forest for him. But he was so upset, he hardly noticed the downpour around him.

All Kyle could think of was what a mistake he'd made by waiting to wed Lily. What kind of a daft fool was he? Her kidnapping had made him realize the depth of his love. He would do anything for his lass, even lose his life for her. She was the sweetest person in all the land, a person who was forever generous, loving, gracious, and beautiful of heart. His priorities had been all wrong. Aye, his job as a Ramsay warrior was important, but not as important as being the husband and protector of Lily of the Ramsays, the true pride and joy of their clan. Aye, their chieftain was the center of the clan, but Lily was its heart and soul.

He loved Lily and she was *his* priority—as his wife, as the mother of his future bairns, as his best friend. And he pledged that he would stop trying to put off their marriage. The moment he found her, they would marry—in the forest, at home, it did not matter where. He would pledge himself to Lily and take her as his wife as soon as possible.

But he had to find her first. *Lord, please help me find Lily.*

It was still pouring, but the thunderstorm was finally letting up. It did not matter, he'd find Cormag through any weather. Up ahead, he heard another horse crashing through the brush. He flicked the reins of his horse, urging him forward.

As he approached a small clearing, Kyle could tell the man on the horse in front of him was indeed Buchan.

"Cormag, you bastard! Where's Lily?" he shouted, pulling abreast of the lout.

Cormag glanced over his shoulder and yelled, "How would I know where Lily is? She's your lass."

Kyle growled and pulled up next to him. Leaping from his horse, he grabbed Cormag and yanked him to the ground in one move. His fist connected with Cormag's face and belly before he allowed the man the chance to speak. "Where is she? I found that foolish cottage you set up for her. I know she was there."

"Aye, 'tis true," Cormag spat. "Lily loves me. She does not want you. I brought her to the cottage because she wished to be away from you. You denied her, so she ran into my open arms. She loves me. I fell asleep with my arms wrapped around her."

Kyle could not believe the words coming from Cormag's mouth. Lies, all lies. They had to be lies. Lily would never have gone with him willingly.

"Filthy liar. If she loved you, then where is she?" Kyle punched him twice more, then threw him to the ground. "Where is she?"

Cormag still refused to answer, so Kyle sat on him, choking him around the neck. "I'll kill you."

Cormag squeaked. "Then you'll never know where she is, will you?"

Kyle hit him in his face, the snap against his fist telling him he had broken the bastard's nose. "Where is she?"

Buchan held his hands up in surrender, attempting to stop the blood pouring out of his nose. "I know not. She sneaked out in the middle of the night. I'm following her as you are. I've lost her tracks in the rain."

A sound echoed through the woods ahead of them, one he did not recognize. Leaving Cormag battered on the ground, he stood up and wandered toward the sound, listening intently, hoping it might provide a clue to Lily's whereabouts.

A wolf. The keening howl of a wolf. A fist punched him square in the gut at the thought of Lily alone in the woods with a pack of wolves. He heard a rustling sound behind him and turned his head in time to see Cormag headed straight for him, his sword aimed for his belly.

Acting on instinct, Kyle unsheathed his sword and swung it in an arc, cleaving Cormag's belly open. Cormag stared at him in surprise just before he crumpled to the ground, the life leaving his body.

It had happened so quickly. Cormag was dead, and he was no closer to finding Lily. Kyle climbed on his horse and moved toward the sound of the wolf, not knowing where else to go. As he made his way through the forest, another sound reached him, one that caused hope to blossom in his heart.

Lily. He could swear he'd heard Lily's voice screaming his name. He moved in that direction, but the undergrowth became too dense, so he leaped off his horse and tethered it to a tree before continuing on foot. He ran through the trees, and though the swinging branches hit him in the side and face, he could not stop. He paused once to yell, "Lily? Where are you? Scream again!"

The wolf howled once more, so he continued to rush through the trees, only pausing when he reached a small clearing in a ravine. He glanced up at the height of the layered stones around him, climbing a small hill toward the sound he'd heard before. Where the hell could she be? There was no sign of aught in front of him but rocks and boulders, shadows of mountains behind them.

His gaze searched the area as he screamed again, "Lily!" He shouted so loud and hard he almost gagged.

Out from behind a rock, standing under an outcropping, came the most beautiful sight he'd ever seen, his Lily.

"Lily, are you all right?" He ran toward her, but came to an abrupt stop as a wolf appeared next to her. There was a snarl on his lips as Kyle edged closer, a snarl that turned to a growl when Kyle lowered his hand to the hilt of his sword.

"Kyle, do not worry."

She reached down to pet the wolf, and his heart leaped into his throat. "Lily, be careful!"

"Kyle, 'tis my friend Moonbeam. I saved him and he has saved me. Come. He'll not bother you." She continued to rub Moonbeam's ear as Kyle took a few tentative steps forward.

Kyle was shocked to see the beast sit back on his haunches, the snarl leaving his face as he nuzzled Lily's hand.

His Lily had tamed a wolf in the wild. He climbed up the slippery slope, grabbing onto rocks and vines to right himself, and when he reached her, she took him by the hand and led him behind the rock and into a cave. She threw herself into his arms as soon as they were out of the rain.

"You came for me. My thanks."

"Of course I came for you. I love you, Lily. Do you know how I've worried? I found that cottage and Cormag."

She played with the folds on his plaid, fixing it and brushing away the dirt. "Beware, Cormag is still out there, and he will probably come for us, but mayhap not until after the rain has stopped."

He watched the woman he loved, noticing how her hands never stopped and her conversation never slowed despite how close she was to falling apart. He stilled her hands before cupping her face. "Lily, Cormag is dead. He will never bother you again. He was the man in the meadow at home and in Edinburgh. 'Tis over, but I'm so sorry I could not stop him from stealing you away."

Tears slid down her cheeks as she gazed at him, her lower lip trembling.

"I love you, Lily. Will you marry me now?"

"I love you too, but I believe you know that. I have always loved you, even when we were wee. But how can we marry now? Out here?"

"Father Rab can marry us as soon as we return, but we can handfast now. I do not care if 'tis not a common practice. It's what's in our hearts that matters. I pledge myself to you, Lily Ramsay. I will always love and protect you." His hand dropped to hers, squeezing it as he waited for her response.

"Oh, Kyle Maule. Aye, I'll marry you. I pledge my heart to you. You are the only one for me."

He took his knife out and cut his thumb, then made a small cut on her hand and placed his thumb over the tender wound. "We are one. You are mine and I am yours, forever."

Lily threw her arms around his neck and kissed him. "Love me, husband. Let us wait no longer."

"With pleasure." He kissed her, tenderly at first to let her know how much he treasured her.

She pulled back and grabbed his hand, "Come see what Moonbeam showed me."

"Moonbeam?"

"Aye, Moonbeam is my new pet."

She tugged him toward the back of the cave.

"Lily, are you sure you know where you are going?" Kyle couldn't help but glance over his shoulder to look for Lily's new pet. Sure enough, the beast was directly behind him. He tried his best not to show any fear of Moonbeam, but he was a wee bit unsettled to have a wolf behind him. "And are you sure Moonbeam doesn't wish for one of us to be his next meal?"

"Aye, I'll tell you about Moonbeam later. First I must show you this." She stepped into another cavern and led the way to a small pool that was illuminated by daylight beaming through a slit at the top of the chamber. She turned around to Kyle and said, "Husband? You need a bath, and 'twill be my pleasure to bathe you."

Kyle's mouth lifted to a quirky grin. "You've been in this water?"

"Aye, I was caught in the downpour just as you were." Grabbing his plaid, she untied it and tossed it off to the side. She reached for his breeches and tugged them off. "I need to see all of you. We must be skin to skin, as is right."

Kyle couldn't believe the fervor with which his wee wife was undressing him. "But Lily, the wolf? I do not know if I can perform with him watching us." He petted the top of the wolf's head, pleased to see the animal accepted his gesture of affection.

"Moonbeam, you must go to the front of the cave to protect us. Do not allow aught to bother us." She leaned down to kiss the top of the wolf's head and rub the soft spot behind his ear, then pushed him toward the entrance. "We'll not be long, and you may join us then."

Moonbeam licked her hand and turned around to do as he was bid. Kyle was dumbfounded, but the sight of his wife dropping her clothing onto the floor brought his attention back to where it belonged.

His mouth went dry when he looked at his wife. "Lily, you are so beautiful." He placed both hands on her hips and tugged her toward him. "I would be lost without you." His lips descended on hers, but this time he ravaged her lips, letting her know how much he wanted and needed her. His mouth angled over hers, their tongues mating, intertwining as their bodies soon would do. His heart beat so fast, he wished he could slow it, but being this close to Lily was more than he'd ever dreamed.

"Kyle, come with me. The water is warm." She took his hand and led him to the edge of the pool, showing him the ledge he could use to ease into the water. He dropped into the pool with a splash, dipping his head under the water and to rid himself of all that had taken place outside. Once he felt replenished, he held his hand out to help Lily into the water.

Lily giggled, watching him carefully. "Are you standing? I did not go in that far before. I was afraid to see what was at the bottom." She was sitting on the ledge now, her long legs dangling in the water.

"The bottom is stone just as the cave is. But I must admit I like you where you are, Lily."

He moved over to her, wrapping his arms around her, melding their bodies together. He kissed her lips, then trailed a path of kisses down her neck, one of her shoulders, and all the way to the underside of one breast, pausing to lift its weigh with one hand so he could explore the entire breast. "You are so soft." His tongue followed the edge of her mound until it found her nipple, teasing it until it became a taut peak.

Lily cried out in response, grasping both hands behind his neck and tugging him closer. "More, please."

Kyle chuckled and took her nipple in his mouth, suckling her until her moans echoed through the cavern. His mouth found hers again, exploring her, teasing her tongue with his, pulsating against her to mimic what he wished to do with her. He wanted all of her, every last inch of her body.

"Do not stop, Kyle, please. I want you inside me."

CHAPTER NINETEEN

"We need not hurry." Her husband whispered. "Enjoy this."

"Nay, I must hurry." Lily did not know how to explain the pressing need inside her, the urgency she felt. She just knew she needed Kyle like she'd never needed anything in her life. "Can you not feel how right we are together?"

She leaned toward him, pressing her breasts against him, the pert mounds now aching for his attention.

Kyle groaned, "Aye, and you force me to lose all control." He hopped onto the ledge, then stepped out of the pond. He gathered the driest of their clothes and formed a soft mound on the cold stone.

He had one dry plaid he'd grabbed from under his saddle to add to the small pile. He helped Lily down onto the makeshift bed before he settled himself above her, resting on his elbows. "My apologies. This will not be as comfortable as it would be on a real bed."

Lily took his hardness in her hand, stroking it the way he liked. "I do not care. I wish to be one with you, Kyle. I love you. We should have done this long ago."

Kyle growled and took her other nipple in his mouth, licking and suckling her until she moaned and called out his name. "Love me more, husband."

His hand teased her sensitive belly before moving down to her nest of curls. Parting them, he found her sensitive spot and caressed her, her hands grabbed his biceps as her whole body thrummed with pleasure.

"You are so wet for me, wife. It excites me to see how much you want me." He kissed her hard on the mouth, and she groaned, teasing him with her tongue.

His hands were doing wondrous things to her, moving inside her until she arched against him and cried out in pleasure. Her legs spread wide, giving him better access. "Kyle, now," she gasped, "Make me yours, please. I need all of you." She brought his sex close to her entrance, but she didn't know what to do. "Kyle?"

Kyle breached her slowly, but it wasn't enough—she wanted him deep inside her. She arched toward him, moving against him, and he growled and thrust deep into her until she felt him cross her barrier. It stung a wee bit, but not enough to make her want to stop.

"Lily, I'll wait until you're ready for me," he groaned.

She did not wish to wait. "I'm ready. Do not stop, please."

Kyle clutched her bottom and drove into her again and again as she urged him on. Lily loved seeing and feeling their flesh twined together like this. Even their sweat was mingling. She pushed against him so that he hit her sensitive spot, teasing her and taunting her with the great release that was to come. Spreading her legs wider, she moaned when she felt him sink deeper inside her, rocking her in a sweet torture that was almost more than she could bear.

He pulsated against her in a keen tempo that caused her to buck against him, making her wish to beg and squeeze him with all she had. He reached down and fondled her spot with a flick of his thumb. She screamed, going over the edge, but she needed more, more, more, so she pushed against him, stroke after stroke, until he stiffened and yelled out as his seed erupted inside her. Her insides spasmed in a sweet ecstasy that she never wanted to end.

It was more than she'd ever thought it could be.

Kyle was humbled by his wife. She'd driven him wild, and he'd lost all control. He'd intended to make this a gentle experience, but he'd been swept away by a passion the likes of which he'd never experienced. "Lily, forgive me for not being more considerate."

"Kyle, 'twas wonderful. You were most considerate of my feelings." She gave him a smoldering look.

Puzzled, he said, "But 'twas your first time. Did it not hurt?"

"Aye, it did hurt a wee bit in the beginning, but not for long. I like it even more than I thought I would. We were meant to be together. Do you not feel it, too?" She ran her finger down his jawline.

He sighed, rolling onto his back and cradling her against him. "Aye, we are meant to be together. I knew it all along, I was just not ready to accept it yet. I thought...och, I know not what I thought. I was a fool, Lily." He kissed her. "We are wonderful together, as you've known all along. I must admit, I've never felt this way about anyone. I love you more than I thought I could."

"Now we can live together forever."

She sighed, a sigh of contentment that exactly expressed his own feelings. As soon as he noticed the blood on them both, he sat up and said, "Come, I'll wash us in the spring."

But just moments after they lowered themselves into the warm water, Moonbeam ran inside, acting agitated.

"My uncle must be here," Lily said.

Kyle bolted out of the water so fast, he almost knocked the wolf over.

"Kyle, what's wrong?"

"Do you not see my ballocks? I happen to like them the way they are. If your uncle is out there, we need to get dressed and quickly.

"But Kyle, we are husband and wife now." Lily followed him out of the water, but he did not stop grappling for his clothes.

"I do not think Logan Ramsay will see it that way. Aye, we shall marry proper as soon as we can, but he may disagree with our reasoning. Please do not discuss what we just shared until after we are married."

Lily laughed as she got dressed. "Kyle, you worry too much. Do you think he and Gwynie waited? Because I would bet he loved her in the forest way before they stood together before Father Rab."

Kyle coughed and grabbed his sword, putting it back in its sheath. "Apparently, you have never been opposite your uncle in a duel of aught—fists, swords, or words. And then there's Aunt Gwyneth who delights in twisting men's ballocks." Sweat beaded on his forehead at the very thought of being at Gwyneth's mercy.

Lily ran ahead of him, but he followed directly behind her. "Lily, I'll go out first. You stay inside the cavern. It may not be your uncle."

"Nay, I must go first. Moonbeam will only do as I say."

Kyle couldn't argue with that, so he stepped back to allow her to go first. "I cannot manage your wolf, Lily. Remind me to ask you about how that came about, will you?"

Lily stopped in front of the big rock at the mouth of the cave. Moonbeam stood growling next to her. "Kyle, 'tis not my uncle."

"Why is Moonbeam growling?" Kyle glanced past Lily and then shoved her back into the cave and drew his sword. At the base of the path stood another wolf, smaller than Moonbeam, and its gaze was fixed on Kyle. "Lily, what do I do?"

Gazing at the brown wolf at the base of the ravine, Moonbeam stopped growling and edged over to stand next to Kyle. Moonbeam howled once and the new wolf charged at them. Kyle flourished his sword, ready to kill if the need arose, but he couldn't get a good read on the situation. Neither wolf appeared to be in an attack stance.

Lily yelled, "Nay, Kyle! I think Moonbeam knows him." She put her arm up to block Kyle's sword arm as they both watched the wolf's approach.

The new wolf stopped short a wee distance from the cave. "Lily, we cannot risk aught. Back inside. Let Moonbeam handle it." He put his hand on the small of her back, and—thank God— she allowed him to guide her back into the cave.

The wolf moved closer to Moonbeam, sniffing him all over before going to his hind leg and sniffing the leg that had been hurt. Then the wolf made the strangest of sounds and nuzzled Moonbeam's neck, and the two fell on the ground together, rolling in a playful game.

"Kyle," Lily clapped her hands together. "'Tis Moonbeam's wife."

Kyle gave her an incredulous look. "You do not believe me?" she asked, looking surprised.

"Do wolves marry, wife?"

Lily groaned. "You know of what I speak. Can you not see that he loves her?"

"I'm not at all certain that it *is* a her. How would you know?"

They watched as Moonbeam and his friend strolled back into the cave and lay down side by side, both of them staring at Lily as she sat on a rock not far away.

"You see? I must find her a name." Lily thought for a moment and then declared, "Starlight. That's what your name is—Starlight."

The wolf stared at Lily, but she clearly did not wish to leave Moonbeam. A low growl erupted from Starlight as she moved to stand in front of Moonbeam, the fur on her neck standing up.

Kyle drew his sword and said, "Lily, if that wolf comes at you, I'll kill it. I do not like this."

Lily held her hand out toward the two wolves and started to sing, a soft tune, the kind that would lull a babe to sleep. As she continued, the wolf stepped back toward Moonbeam, relaxing enough to sit on her haunches. Once the wolf had completely relaxed, indicating it trusted Lily and Kyle, Moonbeam made his way over to Lily and the new wolf followed. They both settled their heads in her lap and stared at her, waiting for her to pet them.

"I've never seen anything like it," Kyle said, stroking his jaw. "My wee wife tames wolves. Have you consulted with them on her new name?"

"Nay, I do not need to. I know she loves Starlight. Look in her eyes, there are stars in the middle of them."

Kyle nodded. "I know not how you come upon your discoveries, wife, but I will no longer question your relationship with animals. Seems they get on with you quite fine."

Lily petted both wolves before kissing each on the forehead. "I'm happy to meet you Starlight."

⁂

They reached Ramsay land later that day. They hadn't met up with any of the Ramsay guards, so Kyle had suggested they head to safety before searching for the others. With Moonbeam and Starlight along with them, he felt a bit more confident with three to guard Lily. He argued that Lily had already been through enough, and she couldn't deny that she wanted to go home. As soon as they rode through the portcullis at the keep, she jumped from Kyle's horse and ran forward, yelling greetings to all.

The first people she ran into were her sire, Uncle Logan, and Torrian, all mounted on horseback.

Uncle Logan and Torrian dismounted to greet her while her father stayed on his horse due to his lame knee.

"Lily? You are hale and hearty?" Torrian held his arms out inviting her into his embrace. "We were just riding out to search for you."

Lily was more than pleased to throw her arms around her dear brother. "Aye, Torrian. I am fine."

A slicing sound rang through the air as two swords were unsheathed in a hurry. "Lily, do not move," Uncle Logan said. "There are two wolves coming up behind you."

Lily laughed as she spun around to face her new friends. Leaning down, she enfolded them in her embrace. "Nay, Uncle. These are my new friends, Moonbeam and Starlight."

Kyle, who had slipped off to take his horse to the stable, giving her a moment to greet her family alone, joined them. "My laird, your daughter has abilities I can hardly understand. I found her in a cave with Moonbeam guarding her."

There was a slight tic to Quade's jaw as his gaze narrowed on Kyle. "And Cormag?"

Kyle cleared his throat before he answered. "Cormag's dead."

"Well done, Maule." Uncle Logan moved to Lily's side to embrace her. "Lily, 'tis most pleasing to see you home again. You've put a hundred more gray hairs on my head, lass."

Lily was surprised at how long her uncle hugged her. When he finally released her, she kissed his cheek, surprised to feel it wet with tears. "I missed you, Uncle."

Kyle grabbed her hand and said, "My lairds, if we may, I'd like a word with both of you.

Torrian glanced at his sire and motioned back toward the keep. "Absolutely, we shall follow you to the hall."

Lily giggled as Kyle dragged her forward. The crowd gave them a wide berth because the wolves followed them, one on each side of Lily as if protecting her.

Coming to a stop, Lily gave Kyle's arm a slight tug. "I need one moment, Kyle." She dropped her hand and ran toward the stable, yelling, "Sunshine, Sunshine!"

She ran down the stables, heading all the way to the outside door at the end. Flinging it open, she yelled, "Sunshine! How I missed you." Before she stepped inside, she motioned for a place for the wolves to wait for her before she went inside. Once they were settled, she moved to her beloved horse, wrapped her arms around her neck, then whispered, "Kyle and I are getting married. Are you not happy for me?"

The horse nuzzled her, but she snorted when the scent of the two wolves must have reached her. "Oh, Sunshine. Those are my two new friends. They can sleep with you if you'd like, but I've left them outside. Their names are Moonbeam and Starlight. I'm sure you will love them as I do."

Kyle came up behind her, then strode over to her horse, petting the horse's flank. "Good to see you again, Tilly."

"Not Tilly, Sunshine," Lily corrected him.

"Sunshine. I suspect Lily will be braiding your mane soon."

Lily threw her hands up toward the sky before wrapping them around Kyle's neck. "Aye, 'tis true. I shall braid your mane, Sunshine, and mayhap I'll put a braid in Starlight's fur. Moonbeam is a lad, so no flowers for him."

"I think you may have to settle for putting flowers on Starlight. I do not think she has enough fur to braid, love."

"I believe you are correct, Kyle. I'll think of some way to make Starlight as pretty as Sunshine. Sunshine will help me, I'm sure."

"I'm happy you've reunited with your horse, but recall your promise to me. We need to find your sire, your brother, and then Father Rab."

"Of course, husband, as you wish." She kissed Sunshine before she hurried back out the door.

They moved past the stables, and Kyle did not slow until they reached the hall. As soon as they stepped inside, he squeezed Lily's hand. Quade, Torrian, her mother, and Father Rab were the only ones inside, and they were all seated by the hearth.

"Mama!" She released Kyle's hand and bolted over to her mother. Wrapping her arms around her, she said, "I missed you so, Mama. I am pleased to be home."

Brenna smoothed Lily's hair and kissed her forehead. "My, but it seems this trip did agree with you, even after the horrible fright we had. 'Tis good to see you home and smiling, lass."

Before Lily could greet anyone else, her sire cleared his throat. "Lily?"

Lily took her husband's hand and glanced up at him, waiting for Kyle to speak. She could feel the sweat on Kyle's palms, but she said naught, giving him the chance to organize his thoughts into words.

"My lairds, I would like to request the honor of marrying Lily, that is, I'd like to make her my wife, if it pleases all of you."

Torrian broke into a broad grin, but he turned to his father to allow him to speak first.

Quade smirked, paused for effect, then drawled, "You've come to your senses finally, Maule?"

"Aye, I love your daughter, and I pledge to honor and protect her forever as my wife, if you please, that is, if you'll allow us..."

Quade stood with his cane, then held his one arm out to his daughter. "Aye, it would please me verra much for you to marry my daughter, but only if 'tis what she wants."

Lily flew into his arms with a happy squeal. "Aye, Papa. We wish to marry soon."

Congratulations were delivered all around, and then Lily and Kyle both turned to Father Rab with expectant faces. "I'd be most happy and honored to conduct this ceremony," he said with a smile. "When would you like to do it?"

"As soon as possible," Kyle said. "I must speak to my mother first."

"Why not at dusk, Father Rab?" Quade said. "'Tis a most lovely time for a wedding. Would that suit you?"

"Must we wait?" Lily asked.

Her mother cleared her throat and ran her gaze up and down Lily's gown.

Lily frowned as she glanced at her dirty mantle, fully aware of the dirty clothes underneath. She had to admit she'd like another bath. "That sounds lovely, Father. Kyle, does this suit you?"

He paused, lost in thought, but then replied, "I am agreeable to this, and we must go speak with my mother. Would you like to go with me? I think she would love to see you."

"Kyle," Quade said, "About your mother..."

Kyle gave him an odd look, but Quade cut himself off and added, "Never mind. Go see your mother."

Lily wished to ask her sire the meaning of his comment, but Kyle was already unsettled. "I would love to visit with your mother."

They left, and Kyle led Lily through the courtyard, his long strides making it difficult for her to keep up with him. As soon as they passed the stables, her wolves joined her, though she noticed everyone else stood far away from them. "Kyle, would you slow your pace a bit, please?"

Kyle said, "Lily, we do not have much time, and your uncle is coming our way. I do not like the look he is giving me. We must hurry."

As they passed her uncle, Lily grinned at him and said, "Greetings, Uncle. We go to visit Kyle's mother."

Kyle nodded in greeting, but he remained intent on his destination.

"Maule, I'd like a word with you," Uncle Logan bellowed after him.

Kyle kept on going as if he'd never heard Uncle Logan. Lily peeked over her shoulder and caught Uncle Logan's smirk, but she decided to let it pass. "Kyle, if you don't slow down, my feet may leave my body."

Kyle stopped to stare at her. "What did you say?"

She pulled on his hand. "Surely you have noticed that my poor legs are not as strong as yours. I cannot keep up with you."

Kyle leaned down to place a kiss on her lips. "My apologies. I needed to get past your uncle, and I think you know why. Did you not hear his bellow? I think he suspects we've handfasted. We are almost at my mother's cottage. What about the wolves? They may frighten my mother."

Lily petted her two friends, but then pursed her lips and tapped her cheek with her finger. After a moment, her face lit up and she leaned down to give Moonbeam a wee push. "Moonbeam, go find something to feed your wife. Surely, you must both be hungry. Then you may return, but please clean up before you do. Kyle and I will be getting married again this eve."

Kyle stared at her, wide-eyed. "And you think he'll understand that?"

Moonbeam took off toward the forest with Starlight directly behind him. Lily threw her arms around her husband's neck. "Aye, I do."

Lily thought they were about to step inside, but they stopped. Kyle gave her a look that almost tore her heart out of her chest. "Kyle, what's wrong?"

CHAPTER TWENTY

Kyle did not know how to explain everything to his wife. He adored Lily, and if he told her what he was thinking, he would hurt her feelings for sure.

He would never do that.

"Kyle?"

How could he tell his wife that his mother might be disappointed to hear of their marriage? Or that his sire would be upset in heaven? With his dying words, his sire had asked him to make him proud by becoming a strong Ramsay warrior and his father must have wanted him to take care of his mama, too. How could he take care of his mother if he was about to move into his own home with his wife? Would his mother expect Lily to move in with them? Would she cry? Though she had asked Kyle about Lily before, claiming she knew he loved her, marriage was different, and this had happened quickly. Mayhap he shouldn't have brought Lily with him when he broke the news.

"Kyle, I think we need to go inside," Lily said, her voice gentle. "'Tis time to tell your mother we will be marrying by sundown." Lily squeezed his hand, and he glanced at the lass he loved.

Aye, it was time. He swung the door open and froze at the unexpected sight in front of him.

Lily pushed him from behind, moving him to one side so she could see what had caught him so off guard.

His mother was wrapped in the embrace of a man, crying on his shoulder.

"Mama?" he whispered.

His mother squealed and raced over to him, throwing her arms around his neck and crying on his shoulder. "Kyle, my sweet lad. You have returned." She cupped his face and said, "I was so frightened I'd lost you." She turned to Lily and wrapped her arms around her. "Lily, I'm so happy to see you safe and home again, too."

The man strode over and clasped his shoulder. "Good to see you again, lad."

"Seamus?" He stared in disbelief at the man who'd been in charge of the Ramsay warriors before he'd taken over for him.

"Aye, 'tis me. We searched and searched for you with no success, then Logan sent us home to see if you'd made it ahead of us. We're so pleased to see you've brought Lily home safely. Well done, Kyle."

"Seamus?" He couldn't get any other words out.

His mother stepped away from Lily, and he noticed that she was working a linen square in her hands. "Kyle, I'm sorry you had to find out this way, but Seamus and I..."

"You and Seamus? How long?"

Seamus wrapped his arm around Kyle's mother's shoulders. "Lad, it has been a long time."

"But why? Why would you hide this from me?" Kyle's mind churned with so many thoughts he didn't know what would come out of his mouth next.

Seamus started to speak, but Kyle's mother grabbed his hand to quiet him. "Nay, Seamus. I'll explain. Kyle, I asked him not to tell you. I know how much you adored your father, and I didn't think you would accept anyone else in his place. Our plan was to wait until you were old enough to handle it, but time got away from us. We should have told you, but by then we were comfortable with the way things were."

Understanding hit him. "This is why you did not wish to move closer to the castle?"

His mother nodded.

He glared at Seamus. "How could you?"

"Kyle Maule," his mother snapped, her tone harsher than he'd ever heard it. "Remember your manners. This would please your father. He would not have wished for me to spend the rest of my life alone."

"Mayhap, but Seamus? He was Papa's best friend. How could

you?" He glowered at Seamus. "And how could *you*?"

"Lad, do not speak to your mother that way." Kyle's mother opened her mouth to say something, but Seamus patted her hand and wrapped it around his elbow. "'Tis time the lad knows." Turning to Kyle, he said, "I'm here at your sire's request, lad. Before he died, he asked me to take care of your mother. I told him I didn't know if I could do it. You see, I was in love with your mother when your father married her. He knew that. He asked me, nay, he told me…" Seamus stared at his feet for a moment before he continued. "Your father told me to marry her. He wished for the two of us to be together."

Tears threatened to spill over Kyle's cheeks. Seamus grasped his shoulder again. "I love your mother, lad. Your sire knew the meaning of a good woman. He had a wonderful one."

Kyle's mother pulled him into a tight hug, something she hadn't done often as he'd grown. "Kyle, I loved your father so. But now I love Seamus. I've found my heart is big enough for two."

The sun seemed to shine a wee bit brighter now that he finally knew the truth. Kyle nodded as a slow smile crept across his face. He kissed his mother on the forehead. "Is your heart big enough for three? We've come to invite you to our wedding at sundown."

His mother squealed again and hugged him. She ran to hug her daughter-in-law to be. "Lily, naught could make me happier than seeing you marry my son." Her hand reached up to her hair. "I must find something nice to wear. Seamus, you must help me wash my hair."

"I'll help you, love."

Kyle clasped Seamus's shoulder. "My thanks for taking good care of my mother, and I apologize for my rudeness."

"Accepted. 'Twas a shock to you. We knew it would be. Know that I am as proud of you as if you were my own son. Now go do what you must to marry our Lily. We'll see you soon."

⁘

Brenna hugged her before they stepped outside into the gray hazy day. "You look absolutely beautiful, Lily. I am so happy for you. You are a glowing bride, my dear."

Lily ran her hands down the over gown she wore. "I have never seen this dress before. 'Tis beautiful."

"Your grandmother made it for you many years ago. It was her way to ensure she'd be here with us in some way. It amazes me how much she understood you at the time. The dress reflects your personality perfectly. I so wish she could see you marry Kyle."

Lily kissed her stepmother's cheek. "She is here, Mama, and so is my first mother. They've told me they will be standing next to Moonbeam and Starlight." Lily picked up the pale blue skirt that had been embroidered with dozens and dozens of flowers, all in different shades. The colors reminded her of her ribbons.

She climbed down the steps and clapped her hands as soon as she saw all her brothers and sisters standing at the base waiting for her. Jennet and Bethia looked so beautiful, Jennet in pink and Bethia in yellow. Gregor looked quite handsome in his blue tartan. After hugging each of her siblings, she ran over to hug Sunshine. She kissed her mare's face and whispered, "You'll only be Sunshine in the future. I know you did not like the name Tilly. I cannot explain myself." She ran a loving hand over Sunshine's carefully braided mane. "Who did this for you, Sunshine? I had hoped to do it, but I did not have time."

Her sisters Bethia and Jennet stood there beaming. Bethia said, "We knew Kyle would bring you back to us safely, so we did it for you."

Jennet added. "Aye, Kyle loves you, Lily. Everyone says so, though I do not understand the meaning of it."

Lily gave her sisters one last hug before she moved over to Torrian. She teared up when she looked at her brother, her kindred spirit for so many years. "Torrian, you look so handsome in your Ramsay tartan. My thanks for all you've done for me."

Torrian gave her a kiss and said, "You and Kyle belong together. You'll have a wondrous life." She leaned over to kiss Gregor, but he held a hand up. "No kisses, please."

Torrian lifted her onto her horse while Bethia helped settle her skirts. They led her through the courtyard and past the chapel. Lily turned sideways, pointing to the chapel. "Torrian, you just passed my wedding."

They all grinned at her as if she were the only one left out of the surprise. Torrian said, "Lily, you are about to see how happy your clan is to have you back and to see you marry Kyle."

Her father sat awaiting her arrival beyond the gates, bedecked in his clan finery and mounted on his horse. How she loved the blue of the dress Ramsay tartan. Sometimes it looked blue and other times it appeared more purple. "Papa, no lad is more handsome than you." He smiled and reached for her hand as they rode side by side toward the end of the meadow. Rows and rows of her clan stood awaiting her arrival, beaming faces and smiles greeting her from every corner of their land.

Lily squealed when they drew close enough for her to see what Torrian had hinted at. They'd chosen a place between two lines of trees at the end of the meadow, and many branches and vines had been interwoven into a long archway overhead, decorated with white flowers, pinecones, and berries. The Ramsay guards lined up on either side of her, all of them dressed in their best, escorting her to Father Rab and her husband. Her mother and Kyle's mother stood off to the side.

As they neared the front of the gathering, Lily's father pulled her closer so he could kiss her cheek, and then Torrian helped her down from her horse and escorted her over to Kyle. Before the ceremony started, Moonbeam and Starlight emerged from the woods and positioned themselves behind her and Kyle, gasps and titters spreading through the crowd at this unexpected addition to the ceremony.

The day could not be more perfect. She gazed up into her husband's blue eyes, thinking about how much she adored him and how happy their life would be. She could hear Kyle's mother crying softly, and a few more people started tearing up in the audience while Father Rab said the words she'd so longed to hear. He wrapped the Ramsay tartan over their hands, representing their union, and Kyle squeezed her hand underneath, smiling at her. He maneuvered his hand so that his sore spot met hers, just as they'd done when they handfasted. How she loved him.

When Father Rab finished, Kyle kissed her deeply, then kissed the cut on the palm of her hand where they'd handfasted. Breathless with excitement, she wrapped her arms around his neck and said, "Catch me, Kyle."

She jumped into his arms and he spun around to face the crowd. "Meet my wife, Lily." He kissed her again, and she cupped his face and said, "I love you, husband."

Once the applause ended and he set her down, she ran over to hug Kyle's mother, Seamus, and her parents. She whispered to her sire, "Papa, may I show everyone?"

He nodded. "If you think you're ready."

"I am, Papa. We've practiced for a long time, and I'd like to show all what I've learned." Her sire kissed her cheek and motioned for Kyle to help her over to her horse, but first she stopped to whisper to Molly, and Molly told her where everything was that she needed.

Lily held her hands up for everyone to be quiet. When she had the clan's attention, she said, "Many thanks for making our wedding so beautiful," she said, gesturing to the archway and the flowers. "This is for all of you. It's also my special thank you to my husband Kyle for saving me." Making her way to her horse, she said, "Come Sunshine, we must perform." She led Sunshine to the middle of the meadow. Moonbeam and Starlight joined her, one falling in on either side of her, and Molly grabbed the ribbon holder that Kyle had created for Lily from its hiding spot and brought it to her in the middle of the field.

Kyle followed her out and helped her up on her horse, giving her a curious look. He whispered, "Promise me you'll not hurt yourself on your wedding day, please?" She giggled and kissed him again, "I promise." Then she announced, "This is for the wonderful gift my husband made for me, and for my papa, who taught me how to do this."

The crowd quieted while Lily rode Sunshine to the end of the meadow. Her heart pounded in her chest, but she was eager to make her sire proud and let her husband know how much she loved him.

She spurred Sunshine to a trot, and as soon as she patted her horse to let her know what she was doing, she placed her bare feet underneath her and did the very thing she'd practiced with her father over and over again.

Lily stood on the back of her horse as Sunshine cantered through the field. Once she felt more confident, Lily lifted Kyle's gift over her head so the braided ribbons streamed behind her in the wind. She sang as they traveled around the field together, Moonbeam and Starlight running beside them.

She stood on her horse's back proudly, just as her father had done when he was young.

Lily was free and in love and married, just as she'd always

dreamed. She belonged here at Clan Ramsay, just as her brother and her sire and her mama and so many others. They had all joined in to make her wedding special and she loved them for it.

She was home.

CHAPTER TWENTY-ONE

After the entire clan celebrated together in the great hall, Logan and Gwyneth ushered the guests out. It had been a long day for everyone, and the family wished to finish their celebration alone. Torrian had moved the Deerhounds into his room to allow Lily's new pets in for the night. She'd promised Torrian to get the pets acquainted over the course of the next few days, though she knew it was possible her wolves would choose to go back into the forest.

Quade motioned for the adults and near adults to move over to the hearth while the youngest went off to their chambers. Once everyone was settled, Logan said, "There are still unanswered questions, and I'd like to have them answered."

"What kind of questions could you have, Uncle Logan?" Lily gave him her most innocent look.

"Kyle has told us what happened with Cormag, but we haven't heard the story from you, Lily. We'd all like to hear about what happened. But first I must ask you both if you learned aught about the Buchans? Did Cormag give you information about his sire?"

"Just that his sire was planning revenge against everyone, not just the Ramsays." Kyle said. "He claimed to have left because he did not wish to take part in what the Buchans were planning." He paused. "And according to him, his sister has gone daft. Whether he was telling the truth, we'll never know."

"I heard something similar about the Buchans from the stable lads at their keep," Molly added. "But they were not planning to come here. They've already lost against our family once. I believe they plan to go deeper into the Highlands."

"Where?" Quade asked.

Logan looked at him and said, "MacNiven used to whisper in

their ear, and I know he was interested in defeating the Grants. My guess is that if they go anywhere, 'twill be after the Grants. I intend to travel there soon to advise them of my suspicions. But enough about them. I'd like to hear how my dear niece got away. What cunning did you use, wee Lily?"

"Of what do you speak? I know not what to tell you." She sat on her husband's lap, cuddling against him.

"How about explaining how you got away from Cormag," Torrian suggested.

His wife Heather added, "Aye, I want to know that, as well."

"I have not much to tell you. You see, when I was in the woods, I discovered something about myself. I have no skills, and I must make amends somehow. Even if I had a bow and arrow, I could not use it against someone, and I'm not as fearless as you, Heather. I could not stab him with a dagger. I was so paralyzed by my fear of being abandoned that I could do naught. If it hadn't been for Kyle, I would not be here."

"Your fear of being abandoned?" Heather asked.

"Lily was kidnapped as a bairn and left up in the trees to die," Logan replied. "'Twas my wife who saved her. Gwynie found her up in the trees and carried her down." Gwyneth sat next to him, so he leaned over to give her a kiss on her cheek.

"I remember it well. I was so frightened to see where she was, and she was so weak." Gwyneth leaned her head on Logan's shoulder.

Lily nodded and then leaned her head on her husband's shoulder. "And I have had terrible nightmares about being abandoned again. It scared me so that I could do naught to help myself."

"But Lily," Brenna said, "you got yourself away from Cormag, did you not?"

"Aye, I did, but 'twas not by fighting or stabbing, I just pretended that I loved him and asked him to go to sleep with me to keep me warm." She turned to Kyle and said, "Forgive me, husband, but 'twas the only way I could get him to leave the door unbarred. You see, he had crafted the lock so that it fastened from the outside. So I had to convince him to come in there with me. I was able to sneak away once he had settled."

Her sire smiled. "Cunning, daughter. That is the skill you used.

I'm verra proud of you. Well done."

Gwyneth agreed. "Aye, I would have fought him and I probably would be dead by now."

Logan held his hands up. "So you've explained how you escaped, and niece, I commend you on a brilliant plan, but I wish to hear about the wolf. How did you manage to befriend a wolf in the wild?"

Lily was still puzzled at being called brilliant and cunning. She couldn't quite understand how her thinking had been cunning. The solution had seemed so obvious to her.

"Daughter?" Quade spoke a little louder than the others. Her papa knew her well—sometimes her mind was far away, and she needed a loud noise to jar her from her thoughts.

"Moonbeam? 'Twas naught brilliant or cunning about it. I found him in the woods pinned under a felled tree. So I used a branch to set him free." She patted his head as if Moonbeam knew they were discussing him.

"Used a branch. Lily, can you not tell us the whole story?" Logan held his hands up, beseeching her to continue.

"I found a long branch, held it under the spot near where Moonbeam was pinned and then pushed on it. It lifted the tree enough to free him."

"And he didn't attack you? He must have been hungry. You have no idea how long he'd been pinned there. Are you daft, niece?"

"Uncle Logan, of course I thought of that. 'Tis why I gave him the huge piece of meat that I'd taken from Cormag's table. I had it in my sack, and I did not need it, so I gave it to Moonbeam before I lifted the tree."

A chorus of groans greeted her pronouncement.

"What?" she asked.

Her sire smiled again, this time with all his teeth. "Cunning again. I'm so proud of you." He glanced at Brenna. "We did not know we'd taught her so well, did we?"

"I had faith in you, Lily." Gwyneth said. "I knew you'd find your way back, or that Kyle would find you."

Kyle added, "And when Starlight came along, Moonbeam snarled at her at first. I wanted to climb the pile of rocks, but Lily was calm as could be. She told me the new wolf was his wife. How she knew that, I'll never know."

They all stared at her as if she had a wolf on her head. What was wrong with her family? Could they not see that Moonbeam and Starlight were natural mates?

"And how did Kyle find you?"

"I refused to give up," Kyle said, running a hand over her hair. "Eventually I heard the howl of a wolf—Moonbeam, here—and then Lily was calling my name."

Torrian chuckled. "Amazing talents, sister. I'm so proud of you, Lily, well done."

Brenna stood and said, "Are you ready for bed, husband? Mayhap 'tis time for us all to get some rest." After saying their good nights to all, Quade joined his wife and headed up the stairs, followed by Logan and Gwyneth.

"Good, now that they are gone, we have a gift for you, Lily. We did not wish for our parents to see it." Molly jumped up to get something, then ran back to hand a package to Lily. "Heather and Sorcha and I worked on this all day while everyone else worked outside."

Lily sat up on her husband's lap so fast that Kyle groaned when he almost dropped her to the floor. She took the gift and played with the ribbon tied around the gift. "You made a gift for me? Just for me? I'm so excited. Kyle are you not excited for me? Should I open it now?"

"Oh, most definitely," Heather replied, failing to hide the smirk on her face.

Lily opened it carefully, and her face lit up as soon as she saw all the bright colors inside. "More ribbons! I love them. My thanks."

Molly's hand hid her smile. "Pull it out of the package so everyone can see it."

Lily pulled it out and held it up for all to see. "How lovely. 'Tis a circlet to wear on my head."

"That circlet is far too big for your head," Kyle said, starting to chuckle.

Heather shook her head. "Nay, this gift is truly more for your husband."

Lily had no idea what she meant by that.

"It is meant to settle over your shoulders."

Lily stood up and settled it over her shoulders. The ribbons cascaded over different areas of her body, but much of her dress was still visible underneath. Molly, Heather, and Gwyneth all burst out laughing.

"Why are you laughing? 'Tis pretty."

"Aye, but 'twas not our intent. You are meant to wear it in your chamber with your husband."

Lily glanced at Kyle. Then she gasped, followed by a giggle.

Kyle still stared at her. Lily leaned over to Kyle and whispered, "With naught on underneath."

Kyle turned the darkest shade of red, so Lily twirled and ran upstairs to her chamber. "I'm going to try it on."

Kyle was directly behind her, the entire family laughing behind them.

He closed the door behind him, bolting it as soon as they entered the chamber they'd been given for the night, leaving Moonbeam and Starlight to lay in front of their door.

"Kyle, help me out of this dress. But first I'll remove the ribbons."

"Naught would please me more than to help you out of that dress. I cannot wait until we have our own cottage."

After Lily removed her gift, she gave her back to Kyle. He untied the ribbons on the back of her dress, then helped her slip out of it so she could remove her shift and stockings.

"Lily, you'll make me a daft man for sure." He reached for her body, but she shoved his hands away.

"Not yet. I want to try my ribbons on."

He groaned but let her have her way. He stood to one side and watched as his carefree wife dropped the circlet over her neck. His mouth went completely dry as he watched her twirl about in the new creation. Who would have thought a bunch of hanging ribbons would be this enticing?

Kyle watched as she lifted her arms over her head and twirled, slowing then speeding up as the ribbons fell between her curves and her valleys, hugging her everywhere. She hummed to herself as she danced across the room, wiggling her bottom until he thought he'd spend himself on the floor in front of her. "Kyle, do you not see how I can make them almost shimmer and wave like the sun?"

"Aye." He closed his eyes. He was so hard under his plaid that he decided to strip himself down as he watched his wife dance for him.

Lily twisted and turned, undulating and swaying to the rhythm of her own music, completely oblivious to the torture she was putting Kyle through. Hellfire, but she was so beautiful, so loving, so genuine. He called her name twice, but she never heard him.

Finally, exasperated, he yelled, "Lily!"

She stopped and stared at him. "What is it, Kyle?"

Frustrated and desperate, he whispered, "I need a hug."

She launched herself at him, wrapping her arms around him and squeezing him.

Lily's skin hit his, and her curves melded to him in a sensual onslaught of everything that was his wife. He kissed her, teasing her tongue until it mated with his. He could feel her nipples peak against him, and he cupped her breast, massaging the soft mound until she moaned. She pulled away, tossed the circlet from her shoulders, and threw herself at him.

They fell onto the bed rolling, each of them panting with desire. Kyle tasted Lily everywhere he could, and the heat and sizzle of her body was almost more than he could handle. Her hands were all over him, on his biceps, on his rigid cock, stroking him, kneading him until he wanted to stop and bury himself in her with one thrust. She pushed him onto his back and straddled him, undulating against his hardness, teasing him with her entrance. Leaning toward him, she offered him her breast and he took it into his mouth, suckling her until she cried out.

Unable to control himself any longer, he grabbed her hips and thrust into her, and she rode him until he thought he would explode. But he wanted them to experience the fullness of their pleasure together, so he held back for her. He teased her sex with his thumb until she went over the edge, screaming his name. He buried himself deep inside her with two more powerful thrusts and let himself go with an orgasm he would not soon forget.

When they were both spent, she fell on top of him, panting, sweating, and smiling. "Husband, 'twas wonderful."

"Wife? Many years ago, you taught me something, and you were so right." He gasped, trying to catch his breath as he caressed her sweet bottom.

"About what?"

"A hug does indeed make everything better."

CHAPTER TWENTY-TWO

Grant land, Highlands

Jake Alexander Grant held up the rear of the line of horses traveling across the glen back to Grant land. His mood was melancholy, though he wasn't sure why. As the firstborn heir to the famous Highland chieftain, Alexander Grant, he had a great future ahead of him, though it would be a long time before his sire was no longer able to lead.

His twin brother Jamie traveled with him along with his cousins, Loki and Kenzie. His sire had sent them out to search the lands for signs of brigands. Reports had told them there were new thieves in the area, but their journey had turned up naught.

They had almost made it home when something called to him. The signal was not loud or clear, but his instincts told him it was not be ignored. He held up the end of the long line of horses coming up through the glen, though he waved the two guards closest to him on ahead.

He stopped his horse.

Not moving, he listened, but there was no sound attached to this nagging feeling. The only thing he heard was his twin brother shouting back to him that the group was riding onward so they could get back to Grant land before the impending rains drenched them. He waved his brother onward, not allowing anything to distract him.

A sound finally called to him off to his left, the faintest rustling from somewhere in the woods, the kind of subtle noise his sire, Alex Grant, had oft warned him to listen for. He climbed off his horse, pulling his sword out of its sheath and moving toward the forest.

The faintest of raindrops could be heard as they hit the leaves still left on the trees. The downpour would start soon, but that same instinct told him he could not leave. Then he caught sight of something hidden on the ground near a bush. It lay completely still, so he doubted whoever or whatever it was still lived. Hell, but he hoped it wasn't a dead body. He did not handle death well.

Jake held his breath as he leaned in to pull more branches back, but the sight before him made him gasp aloud. He bent down on one knee to get a closer look. He let out a low whistle when he saw a trim ankle, dusky colored, jutting out from the lump of material.

He'd seen women beaten before but this, this…was way beyond anything he'd ever seen. He was so undone by the sight of her, his hands moved automatically without needing any specific directions. Moving the dirt and leaves off the lass, he scooped her into his arms to pick her up.

Dark red locks, dirty and matted, fell away from her face as he lifted her into the air. He had no idea what color her eyes were beneath her long lashes, but her porcelain skin had a dusting of freckles across her nose and delicate cheekbones, though the swelling indicated one of them might be broken. Long pale legs hung over his arm, so covered in blood that her clothing stuck to her in various places.

He lifted her skirt just to see the extent of her injuries, and his reaction was immediate. Dropping the fabric, he gagged, turning his head to the side because he thought he might heave all over the ground. Who could treat a lass so?

Once he recovered, he moved toward his horse, whistling for his brother to return to assist him. While he waited, he held her close as an overwhelming need to protect her descended on him. He vowed to find the whoreson who did this and make him pay. His honor as a Highlander demanded it of him. It was such an all-consuming need that he did not care if his clan would help him right this wrong. He'd take this on by himself, if need be.

He held his ear down to her mouth and heard her shallow breathing. She was still alive, but for how long?

He settled his forehead against hers and closed his eyes before he whispered, "I'll protect you, lass. You have my word."

EPILOGUE

The following year

Kyle paced the great hall.

The love of his life was in a chamber above stairs with Lady Brenna, giving birth to their first son or daughter. He ran his hand down his face, pacing the hall for the hundredth time. "How long does this process take? Must she torture me like this?" He threw his arms in the air for emphasis, hoping the angels watching over his wife would see his frustration and take pity on him.

Logan and Quade sat in front of the hearth, drinking ale. Quade said, "I recall one lass who took two days to deliver her bairn. I did not think my wife would ever return."

"Two days? Truly? I'll not survive it if Lily takes that long. Can you not hear her scream? She'll be the death of me by the end of the day."

Logan laughed. "She's not screaming that much. Gwyneth screamed so loud when she popped Gavin out that Seamus came running in from the lists."

Gwyneth smacked her husband's arm as she passed him, coming from the kitchens with a few pieces of fruit. "If you recall, I was yelling at you. I said you'd never touch me again. Stop scaring the lad."

Logan jumped out of his chair to waylay his wife. He nuzzled her neck and grabbed her hips. "Seems my touch pleases you again, aye?"

She laughed, shoving at him. "Aye, but we've not had another bairn since, have we?"

"Aye, we have. You do not recall making Brigid?"

Gwyneth halted at the top of the stops. "Seems you have the right of it. 'Twas a wonderful daughter we made."

Logan growled as he chased up the stairs after her. "Since you're headed in the right direction, I'll follow. We can make another."

Gwyneth spun around and planted her hands on her hips at the top of the stairway. "I doubt that shall ever happen again. We're both too old. Now go back down the stairs and console your nephew. I'm needed by our dear niece."

Logan returned to the hall, stopping to pat Kyle's back as he passed him. "Lily is a strong lass. She'll be fine. Her mother is in heaven watching over her. Come sit for a bit." He ushered him over to a chair.

Kyle sat, rubbing his hands up and down his legs. He'd heard too many nightmare stories about lasses dying birthing bairns, or delivering a bairn that had something wrong with it, or delivering a dead bairn, or...

Quade said, "Stop thinking of the worst, Kyle. You'll insult my wife's abilities to deliver the bairn safely."

Kyle stared at his father-in-law, but he could not quite summon the energy to lie to him, so he said nothing. Lily had been in there for at least six hours. "But how can she keep going? She must be exhausted. Will she have the strength to push the bairn out after working for so long? I do not understand how this works. How can a lass live through all that pain? 'Tis gruesome to listen to them."

His feet bounced against the floor, shaking his whole body.

Quade peered at the ceiling. "I've never understood it, to be honest, how the Lord could torture a woman so. But watching a loved one deliver a bairn is mighty painful, too. It can bring the most powerful man to his knees."

Kyle pondered this thought before he peered at his father-in-law. "My laird?"

"You're in our home, Kyle. Call me by my given name, please."

"As you wish. Quade, may I ask you a personal question?"

"Aye, I'll answer if I'm able."

"Lily's mother. She died birthing Lily, 'tis true?"

"Not quite. She died from the act of giving birth. Something went wrong after Lily's birth. She did not die until some time later."

"How can you sit there so passively? How are you not banging on the door to see if your daughter is doing well? Are you not afraid the same will happen to her?"

"Well, 'struth is that it has crossed my mind a few times, but my daughter has a much more skilled midwife caring for her than Lilias did. I have great faith in Brenna. 'Tis her daughter in her hands. She'll see her through."

Kyle stared at the floor in front of him.

"Lad, you'll see the Lord acts in strange ways. He took one wife from me and then gave me another. I love them both. Brenna has been a Godsend for my clan, so I do not question his ways. A part of me feels certain Lilias brought Brenna to us. Brenna cured her son and daughter of their illness. Nay, I do not question any more, son. I've seen too much."

The door to the great hall opened and Kyle's mother came in with Seamus. "Kyle? Is Lily all right? Has she had the bairn yet?"

Kyle escorted his mother to a chair by the hearth. "Nay, Mama. She's in the chamber above stairs."

Quade added, "She's torturing your son. He's been waiting a while."

"Kyle, the first bairn takes a long time. I cannot wait to see if you have a lad or a lassie." She clasped her hands together in her lap. "Seamus and I shall wait with you, no matter how long it takes."

"My thanks, Mama. I just want them both to be hale and hearty."

Logan said, "I believe they'll be fine. Lily is a strong woman. Remember how she found a way to escape a daft man on her verra own. Your wife is strong."

Kyle suddenly bolted out of his seat. "What is happening?"

Logan gave him a strange look, tipping his head to the side. "Kyle? I do not hear aught. What do you hear?"

"I hear naught and 'tis wrong. She promised to sing every so often so I'd know she was hale. I've heard naught for too long." He charged up the staircase, taking them three steps at a time. "Lily?"

A grated voice singing out of tune met his ears. "Ramsay land is…"

Kyle waited, but the chamber went silent. "Lily, Ramsay land is what?"

A loud yell came from the chamber. "Is bonny land. Go downstairs, Kyle!"

Scowling, he retraced his steps back down to the hall and resumed his pacing.

Not long after, Torrian and Heather came in the front door, their first born son strapped to Torrian's chest. Nellie came in behind them. "Where's the new bairn?"

Kyle stared at the three of them, unable to answer, and continued pacing.

The group started to chatter, and the noise was loud enough that he didn't notice the silence from the chamber above stairs until the door opened.

"Kyle?" Gwyneth yelled over the balcony railing. "Would you like to come in?"

He flew up the stairs and pushed past Gwyneth, desperate to see his beautiful wife again. "Lily?"

Lily sat up in her bed, a huge smile on her face and a small bundle in her arms. "Come closer, Kyle. Meet our daughter."

Kyle grabbed a stool and moved it by the bed, leaning in to kiss his wife before he sat on the stool. "We have a wee lassie?"

She nodded and pulled the plaid back so Kyle could peek at the bairn. "Is she not beautiful, Kyle? Look, she has your dark hair."

Kyle smiled as soon as he saw their daughter. Her face was all scrunched up in preparation to bellow, and her wee fists flailed around her as she opened her eyes to her new world. "Lily, she's beautiful. You'll not die on me now, will you?"

Lily smiled. "Nay, everything was perfect, right, Mama?"

Brenna smiled at the end of the bed, fussing with her tools. "Aye, Lily came through it beautifully. We had only one surprise."

Kyle glanced back at their daughter, still infatuated with the new one. He reached for her hand, and the lass grabbed onto his finger, opening and closing her mouth. "She looks as if she's about to start hollering about something."

A scream echoed through the room, but not from the bairn in front of him. He jerked his head to a spot in the corner. In a basket sat another bundle, the source of the second yell.

Kyle sat up wide-eyed, glancing first at Brenna, then Gwyneth, then his wife. All had wide smiles on their faces, but none of them spoke.

"What?" he whispered, squeezing Lily's hand.

A knock sounded at the door as Gwyneth reached down to the basket. Quade opened the door and peeked in while the other members of their family waited behind him. At the same time Gwyneth picked up the second bundle.

"Greet your other daughter, Kyle. You have two wee lassies."

Quade whistled and clapped his hands. "Twins! You've blessed us this day, dear Lord!"

Logan hopped in the air, declaring, "Two wee Lilys! Thank the Lord above. What more could we ever ask for?"

Nellie cried, "I was hoping they'd be lassies."

Kyle glanced from bundle to bundle, then fell off his stool backwards, passing out cold.

The End

NOVELS BY KEIRA MONTCLAIR

DEAR READERS,

I hope you enjoyed my third novel in The Highland Clan series. If you enjoyed reading about Lily, her story began in *Healing a Highlander's Heart*, and her trouble "in the trees" happened in *Highland Sparks*. I think you know that Jake's story will be next, and you can count on the fact that I have many more stories to tell in The Highland Clan. There could be more than thirty in this series if I tell all the bairns' stories! I have a third Summerhill story started, also.

If you want to know more about my novels, here are some places for you to visit.

1. Visit my website at www.keiramontclair.com and sign up for my newsletter. I'll keep you updated about my new releases without bothering you often.

2. Go to my Facebook page and 'like' me: You will get updates on any new novels, book signings, and giveaways. https://www.facebook.com/KeiraMontclair

3. **Stop by my Pinterest page:** http://www.pinterest.com/KeiraMontclair/ You'll see how I envision Lily and Kyle.

4. Give a review on Amazon or Goodreads. Reviews help self-published authors like me and help other readers as well.

Happy reading!

Keira Montclair
www.keiramontclair.com

ABOUT THE AUTHOR

Keira Montclair is the pen name of an author who lives in Florida with her husband. She loves to write fast-paced, emotional romance, especially with children as secondary characters in her stories.

She has worked as a registered nurse in pediatrics and recovery room nursing. Teaching is another of her loves, and she has taught both high school mathematics and practical nursing.

Now she loves to spend her time writing, but there isn't enough time to write everything she wants! Her Highlander Clan Grant series, comprising of eight standalone novels, is a reader favorite. Her third series, The Highland Clan, set twenty years after the Clan Grant series, focuses on the Grant/Ramsay descendants.

You may contact her through her website at www.keiramontclair.com. She also has a Facebook account and a twitter account through Keira Montclair. If you send her an email through her website, she promises to respond.

Made in the USA
Middletown, DE
10 October 2017